A Mysterious Winged Figure

Kara was about to run, but was interrupted by a sudden rush of wind as something huge swooped down low overhead. The thieves did not seem to notice, but the robed stranger did. He hissed in fury. "The sky! He is here! Fire!"

All the robed figures brought out things from under their robes—rifles. The thieves fled as the robed men began firing wildly into the black sky. It was deafening. The corpse man brought out a rifle as well and used it with a more studied aim. Kara caught a glimpse of one milky white eye. She clapped both hands over her ears and ran, along with the other thieves, for cover, for safety. A muffled gasp came from above, and something wet fell on her hand. She squinted at it and saw black droplets. She ran faster, losing herself in the night.

The Alarna Affair

written and illustrated by

Ruth Lampi

The Five Wits Press
Philadelphia, Pennsylvania

Copyright © 2010 Ruth Lampi

*To my two families,
the Lampis who bore me and read out loud to me,
and the Van Oorts who let me come share in their adventures.*

All rights reserved. No part of this publication may be reproduced or transmitted by any means without written permission from the author.

Cover art by Ruth Lampi
Design and editing by Jessica Van Oort

ISBN 978-1-4507-2511-8

Printed in the United States on tree free 30% PCW recycled paper produced with 100% wind energy

www.worldofshandor.com

Contents

1. The Remarkable Professor Sheridan — 1
2. A Daring Theft, and a Most Mysterious Apparition — 8
3. An Unexpected Passenger — 15
4. Introducing the Blackfeather Family — 20
5. The Discovery of the Guardians' Door — 29
6. The Return of Doctor Blackfeather — 40
7. Thieves in the Night — 48
8. What Amazing Events Can Transpire in Half an Hour — 53
9. A Rooftop Chase and a Grim Revelation — 60
10. A Marvelous Secret Revealed — 71
11. Into the Tomb — 83
12. What Was Found on the Warrior's Grave — 91
13. Against a Terrible Foe — 99
14. Concerning Gifts and Legacies — 110
15. A Few Words in Parting — 119

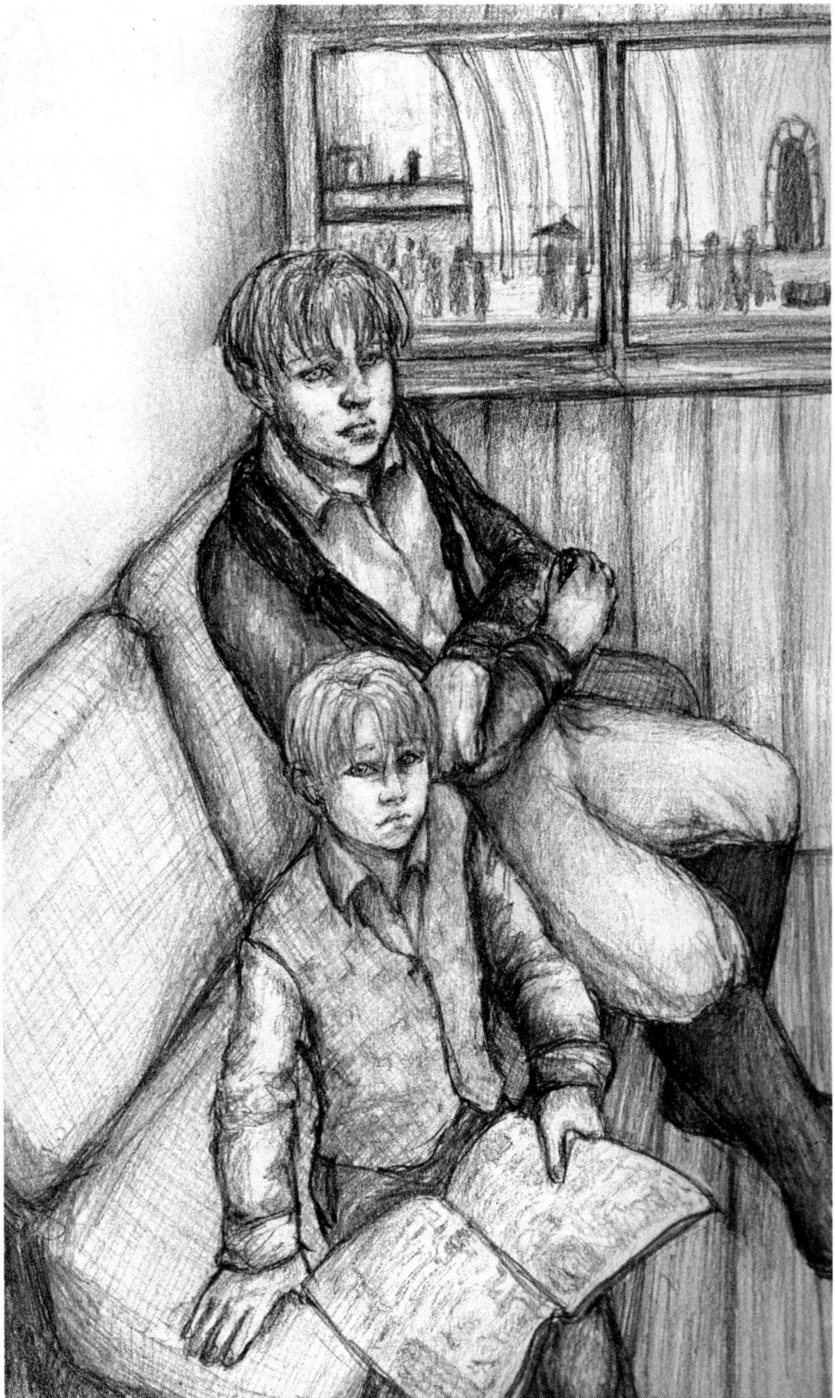

Chapter One
The Remarkable Professor Sheridan

"The train is stopping. I think we're here," Jon Gardner told his brother Tam.

Tam leaned over to join Jon in peering out the compartment window at the gray, misty view outside. The train gave out a loud hoot and one long, slow lurch that sent the luggage sliding beneath the seats, and then it was still. The mist outside parted to reveal a busy platform with bustling porters and passengers.

"Those are fine horses," Tam observed, squinting out at the road beyond the station where bright carriages passed to and fro. "Don't know about those carriages though. Gaudy."

One gilt carriage stopped to let out an especially gaudy set of foreigners in fine clothing. Porters scrambled to carry a great array of boxes and trunks from the carriage to the train. One porter dropped the end of an enormous trunk and a foreign man in a top hat waved a cane and shouted at him.

"You don't think Professor Sheridan is with them, do you?" Jon asked, suddenly a little nervous.

"Nah." Tam rubbed at his nose. "The professor's a good honest Shandorian, right, like us. We've no use for gilt carriages."

"I think we should get out and have a look round. I want a paper. I bet they have papers here. New ones, from today even." Jon peered about, looking for shops, or for the boys who had gone around waving papers at the last stop.

Tam, sandy haired and big framed, leaned back in his seat and frowned. "That's nonsense. It's best we stay right here where the Professor can find us. I won't be losing you in that crowd." Tam caught his brother's disappointed look. "And who's to say you could read the papers here? They might be foreign."

"We're in Vellinos. They're bound to speak trade common here. We're just south of Arien. They might get the *Arienish National Times*."

"You've got one of those in your case already," Tam pointed out.

Jon sighed. "But Tam, it isn't new. They make a new one every week."

Tam shrugged. Tam could read, he just didn't care to, not like Jon did. A puff of steam outside obscured the view from the window and showed Jon his own reflection briefly in the glass. A thin boy with large blue eyes looked back at him, his blond hair cut neatly short, his best clothes rumpled from several days' travel. He was not wearing the cravat his mother had carefully tied onto him. Jon looked about for the thing. Should he be wearing it to meet the Professor? The Professor was famous, after all, and Mother had wanted Jon to make a good impression. His essay had certainly made enough of an impression to win him this great opportunity: a summer working with Professor Eabrey Sheridan at the archeological dig site in Alarna, along with the equally famous and even more mysterious Doctor Corin Blackfeather. Jon found the cravat wedged between two seat cushions and pulled it free to find it was a wrinkled mess.

The window was clear again and Tam was looking outside now, with the familiar dubious expression that said he wasn't comfortable in strange and foreign parts. Tam had come along to look after Jon, and for no other reason. At nine, even a very mature and intelligent nine, Jon Gardner was not permitted to travel alone, but with thirteen-year-old Tam along, big for his age and steady, Mother trusted they would get safely to the Professor's watchful eye. She had left Tam with all kinds of instructions, and he was taking them quite seriously.

"I don't like the look of that fellow," Tam muttered, frowning at the crowd of folk now boarding the train. Jon looked, but saw no one especially suspicious.

"Too pale," Tam explained. "Like he's never seen the sun or plowed a field. The man behind him is as dark as honest dirt. He seems all right. He didn't object when the rude, pale fellow butted in line."

"The pale fellow is Arienish, I think." Jon said. "Nobility maybe."

"Don't see nothing noble about him," Tam said. "He needs some sun. And he's wearing gloves. What kind of man wears little white gloves?"

"It must be a fashion," Jon said. The Shandorian fashion for men consisted of a sturdy work shirt, breeches, suspenders, and a vest and jacket. Jon's jacket, folded in the corner for a pillow, was grayish blue. Tam's, slung over an open valise, was brown. Mother had let Tam's coat out recently to make more space in the shoulders. The new cloth was a little darker than the old.

"Is that the Professor, do you think?" Tam pointed out an elderly fellow with enormous whiskers in a trim dark coat. Jon looked him over, but wasn't sure.

"Maybe that fellow." The next man was dark skinned, in a big coat, and carrying a large valise. "Him, maybe?" Tam pointed out another man with a beard, but he moved a step to reveal a family in company with him, noisily boarding the train.

"Pardon me," a soft adult voice spoke from the door behind them. "But am I correct in assuming that you are Tam and Jon Gardner?"

The boys turned to find a young man at the door of their compartment, looking in. He was an adult, but not much taller than Tam, and carrying only a single worn satchel. He had calm eyes, an awkward smile, and long blond hair pulled back in a tail. His clothes were somewhat old-fashioned and showed signs of wear at the cuffs and hem. He wore tall leather travel boots, like the northern clans in Shandor did, but also a hat of an Arienish fashion. Most peculiar of all, the man's young face, and his hands and neck as well, were webbed over with a faint tracery of old scars. Jon wondered what had happened to him. Without the scars, the man would have been considered handsome. The man smiled at them, a little nervously, and took off his hat. "I'm Eabrey Sheridan. That is, Professor Sheridan, if you like. You *are* the Gardners?"

"We are, sir, and it's good to see you, sir." Tam rose and shook the Professor's hand heartily. Jon shook the scarred hand next, suddenly speechless in the presence of the man who had been his idol for some years. Jon was very surprised to find the Professor so young. For a man with five doctorates, who had written over nine volumes and hundreds of essays, he was not at all what Jon had expected.

The Professor seated himself on the cushions Tam hurriedly cleared of stray luggage, and Jon continued to stare at the famous scholar, unable to help himself. The Professor's ears, revealed now that his hat was at his side, were a curious shape, like leaves, and came up through his long hair. There was scarring there too, but like the rest, old. Jon tried to ignore all the spidery light lines of scars and focus on the man's blue eyes. "It's an honor to finally meet you, sir," he said. "I've read all your books."

The Professor raised his eyebrows and smiled again, mildly. "I hope they didn't bore you. My students tell me I have a long winded and old-fashioned way of rambling when I get too involved in a topic."

"I liked your books, sir. I especially liked what you had to say about the inscriptions discovered under the castle in Shandor, and your translations of the Ancients' text there. I believe you are right in thinking that the wing rune describes an entity rather than an action."

The Professor looked surprised and pleased. "I look forward to hearing what you think of the text found in the ruins at Alarna, then. I'm eager to see it myself."

"Has Doctor Blackfeather offered a translation?" Jon asked.

"He is waiting for us, and for some papers I've brought with me." The Professor gestured toward his satchel. "I have been studying the legends and history of the site to try and get some idea of what we might find at the dig. Most scholars agree that Alarna was once the center of a great civilization. They used bronze weapons and had superior skills in masonry, with which they built great cities and temples. Certain texts mention that Alarna was ruled by an immortal god-king who conquered many neighboring lands. He was a harsh, cruel ruler who demanded many sacrifices. One day a great warrior from an unknown land slew him and brought his temple crashing to destruction with all his wealth and glory in it."

"So we might be digging for buried treasure?" Tam asked.

"Likely not." The Professor smiled apologetically. "The

tomb robbers of Alarna are famous for their exploits. Any treasure will be long gone, but we hope to find clues to what really happened between the warrior and the god-king. If we can discern the events of that encounter, it may have some bearing on other, er, historical encounters with which Doctor Blackfeather and I are concerned. In studying." The Professor brushed some unseen dust from his worn trouser knees, looked up, and smiled at Jon. "What I find *most* fascinating is that Doctor Blackfeather's expedition has found writing of the Ancients on a tablet at the Alarna site."

The Ancients, Jon knew, had lived in Shandor long ago. They were the people who had built the foundations of the castle and left artifacts, stories, and traces of their bloodlines to Shandor's people.

"As you likely know," the Professor said, "it is rare indeed to find their written language anywhere outside of Shandor."

"Uh," said Tam. "Right. Old writing."

Jon smiled at his brother's bewildered look, and then at the peculiar Professor Sheridan. It was wonderful to finally meet someone who could speak the same language of old civilizations, ruins, and stories. Tam was a good brother, but his interests were all in horses, farming, and the soil of Shandor, not for its history but for its everyday present. "Professor Sheridan, can you tell us more about the ruins at Alarna? Is it true there are underground rivers, and that they found a gallery of tombs with the people encased all in painted clay?"

Tam was asleep before an hour had passed. The conversation paused only long enough for the three to have dinner from the supper cart, hours later.

"How long will it be until we reach Alarna?" Tam asked that

evening.

"Two days," the Professor replied. "Tomorrow we switch trains at the grand terminal in Merigvon and take the southern line down overnight to an outpost station in Alarna. We'll travel by carriage from there, out to the dig."

Tam sighed. "We've already been on the train four days. I didn't know you could be so far from home. How many days would it take to walk back, do you think?"

Jon thought. "Over a year, probably, unless you had wings."

Chapter Two
A Daring Theft, and a Most Mysterious Apparition

The grand terminal at Merigvon could be seen from some distance, gleaming amid the city's spires. The great glass roof seemed to slide arching over them like a glittering clamshell as the train pulled slowly in. Other trains passed quite close to them, alarming Jon until he remembered they were all on their own tracks and couldn't possibly collide.

Dozens of tracks led into the cathedral-like building, and trains of all kinds stood puffing and steaming under vaulted arches of steel, stone, and glass. Statues stared down grimly from the high ornamented arches and balustrades on either side of the hall. Cherubs, soldiers, and ladies in flowing robes with scrolls and baskets of fruit were everywhere upon the high walls. Stone wreaths and angels, memorials of some foreign war, stood at the east end of the hall, winding around the largest clock Jon had ever seen in his life. The Gardner boys regarded the place with wonder, faces pressed close to the window.

"This is the crossroads of the continent," Professor Sheridan informed them, straightening his hat carefully. "We will change trains here, and be able to stretch our legs."

"Do they have papers?" Jon asked, hearing his own voice rather smaller and more breathless than he wanted.

"Quite a few. I telegraphed ahead to have certain titles bundled and ready for my arrival. We shall have a pile of reading for the next leg of our journey."

Jon returned the Professor's smile readily.

Tam insisted on carrying both cases of luggage—Jon's,

heavy with books and papers, and his own lighter case with the broken handle that had to be held just so. Professor Sheridan, as before, carried only his satchel.

As they stepped down off the train Professor Sheridan checked his pocket watch against the large clock on the eastern wall and satisfied himself that it was correct. He slipped the watch back into a frayed pocket of his waistcoat. "Come along. Let us see if we can brave the crowd and find some tea before our train comes in."

Tam followed after the Professor, lugging both cases, and Jon tried as best he could to keep up, despite the crowd pressing all around. He heard Tam mutter something about more people than he'd ever seen, but then his brother's voice was drowned in the howl of steam from a train pulling out. A man in a heavy fur shoved past Jon, pushing him sideways, and he lost sight of Tam and the Professor. Jon had a frightening moment trying to find them again while caught behind a large procession of porters pulling along big carts of luggage. He was pushed first to one side then another, but found himself at last carried along to an archway where a very panicked looking Tam and the calmer Professor were waiting for him.

"You hold to my coat now," Tam ordered. "I'd have you hold my hand but I can't with the cases. One of those luggage men tried to take them from me, if you'll believe it. I won't go letting someone else carry our things to who knows where. You stay close now."

"Why don't you walk at my side?" the Professor suggested.

He ushered them carefully through a small maze of galleries full of shops, and up an ornate iron stair to a tea shop, where he settled the boys at a table on a balcony overlooking the terminal. He ordered tea and cakes for two, then stood. "I will be back in a moment. I'm going to pick up those papers."

The boys were able, from the vantage of the balcony, to admire the great terminal at their leisure.

"This is as big as the Great Hall in Shandor, maybe," Jon said.

"Nah. The Hall is higher," Tam insisted, looking impressed nonetheless.

"Look at all the trains. I bet you could travel anywhere in the world from here."

"Not to Shandor you couldn't. You have to go on good honest horseback all the way from Sherard station to get to Markerry and out to our farm. We don't need trains back home."

Jon remembered the horse ride to the first train station fondly, but he liked the trains just as well. "I wonder what the next train will be like. Maybe there will be even more cars this time. The Professor says some trains have dozens of cars. That one down there has twenty-three."

"The next train will be like our last train," Tam grumbled, rubbing his back. "Rumbly, fast and loud. You'd think a thing going on two rails could travel smooth."

The tea came then, with an assortment of little cakes that neither brother could find any reason to grumble about.

"Ought we to save some for the Professor?" Jon wondered, a little too late, looking at the single cake remaining.

"I've the money from Mum. I'll stand a second course if he wants some," Tam decided. Comforted by this decision, they split the last cake between them. The Professor appeared a moment later, carrying in both arms a bundle of papers so thick it made Jon's heart leap. The Professor insisted on paying the bill, over Tam's protestations, though when Tam saw what the bill *was* for tea and cakes for two at the grand terminal he turned a little pale. "Please, gentlemen," the Professor said, "you are both my guests." With that he ordered a box of the cakes to take along, and gave them to Jon to carry for safekeeping.

They wound their way back down the staircase and out into the crowd again. Jon was very careful to stay close beside Professor Sheridan, and so it was that he saw the dark ragged boy in the oversized coat deliberately bump into the Professor and snatch his pocket watch.

Jon cried out indignantly. The urchin regarded him with cool defiance, and just as suddenly as he had appeared, he dashed off into the crowd with the Professor's watch in hand.

"Thief!" yelled Jon. Tam had seen it too, and he dropped the cases and took off after the boy, bellowing.

The Professor lifted a hand and seemed about to say something when an ill-shaved man behind him pulled suddenly at his satchel, setting the Professor off balance and sending the bundle of papers falling to the floor. The man pulled the satchel from the Professor and ran in the opposite direction, leaving a scene of chaos behind him.

The Professor shouted for the station guard and seemed torn for a moment whether to chase the second thief or stay with Jon. Some station guards saw the man running and gave chase. Professor Sheridan frowned, sighed, and began gathering his scattered bundle of papers. Jon stared, distressed, after the man fleeing with the satchel who raced across some open tracks just ahead of a train that was pulling in. As he disappeared behind the moving train, something huge and dark swooped by overhead, sending up a gust of wind along with the rush of air from the train.

Jon stared, looking up as a winged figure in flowing black plunged down from amid the ranks of statuary and swooped low over the crowd. The figure's wings were big and black, the span of a train car's length. The face, only briefly glimpsed, was a man's, unearthly beautiful and calm, still as a statue, with terrible, strange, burning eyes. He was there and gone in an instant, sweeping over the moving train and diving to ground on the opposite platform, invisible now along with the thief. Jon stared around open-mouthed to find the crowd already calming, oblivious to what he had just seen. No one looked up, pointed, or seemed in the least alarmed by the sudden gust of wind kicked up by giant wings.

The train that obscured the thief and the apparition finished pulling out and the opposite platform was visible, empty of anything interesting whatsoever. There were no thieves or winged figures to be seen.

"Did you see? Professor, there was . . . are you all right, sir?" Jon looked down anxiously at the Professor, who was on the ground again, not fallen, but retrieving the last of his papers, and one large ebony feather.

The Professor examined the feather with keen interest and glanced up and around, as if looking for something. His brow smoothed and he tucked the feather carefully into an inner pocket of his coat. He rose and dusted off his coat, visibly collecting himself, then lifted his eyebrows in a look of mild apology to Jon. "Quite a day. But there's no real harm done. We have the important things." He hefted the papers and nodded at Jon. "I see you still have hold of the cakes. That's lucky. Let's see if we can retrieve your headstrong brother."

"But Professor, your notes, your research!"

"All in my head, as strong as on paper," the Professor assured, oddly calm.

Jon admired the man very much for holding together appearances for his sake, but felt the Professor must be very upset about losing all his research, not to mention his possessions. "But you've been robbed."

"It happens," the Professor answered. "But this time nothing of great importance has been lost. See, here's your brother."

Tam jogged back to them, panting. "That little pickpocket was fast. He got away from me. I'm sorry, sir."

"A man stole the Professor's satchel!" Jon told him.

"Bloody foreigners!" Tam cried, aggrieved. "What kind of place is this?"

"It's all right," the Professor said, his voice still calm and soft. "Let us find our train, gentlemen, before we have any other misadventures."

Tam caught up the cases and gripped them firmly, looking suspiciously from side to side as he followed close on the Professor's footsteps. Jon hurried along beside him. "Tam, did you see . . . anything unusual, while chasing that boy?"

"Not unless you count a great lot of clumsy foreigners."

"You didn't see, well, anything that looked like a living statue, did you?"

"No. Why?"

"No reason. I just thought I saw something." Jon frowned at the Professor's back and thought of the feather he had picked up. But the Professor hadn't looked up when the winged figure had passed over, or noticed the wind. No one had seen the man with wings but Jon. *I know I saw that*, Jon thought. *Why didn't anyone else?*

Chapter Three
An Unexpected Passenger

The Professor and his charges boarded their new train without further incident. It was bigger than the last train and painted green, with brown upholstered bench seats in little walled compartments. A hallway beside the compartments ran the length of the passenger cars, of which there were sixteen. The eight luggage cars and six freight cars were all off limits to passengers. There were also three dining cars, two for the more well off passengers and one for everyone else.

The boys had explored all they were allowed of the train in a very short time, found the nearest lavatory, and chosen how they wanted to sit in their own compartment. The Professor remained remarkably calm about the loss of his watch and satchel. Jon wanted to ask him about the feather, but felt it would be impolite. The Professor was being so very kind to them. Unlike other grown-ups, it didn't matter to him who read what paper first, and so both boys were invited to share freely in the wealth of words before them.

Tam was at first reluctant to touch the things, but in a little while he found a story serialized in the *Arienish National Times*, of which there were three issues collected. He began to work his way through it slowly, mumbling half aloud to himself in sections.

Jon was delighted to find that seven of the papers were in trade common and two were in Levour, which he could read fairly well, having learned it in the last year. Two more were in Germhacht, another language he could read passably. The Professor read from some paper in a queer alphabet that he explained was Corestemarian.

At length Tam reached the end of the *Times* without reaching the end of the story, and snorted with disappointment. "It was a ridiculous story anyway," he said. "The lady kept having fainting fits at the least thing, and all the folk used too many words to say what they meant. If people really went on like that it would be a crazy sort of world."

Jon grinned behind his paper. He had found a fascinating piece about some archeologist's finds in the southern continent that contented him for some time until at length even he got restless. Later in the afternoon he took a stroll up and down the hallway and a made a game of keeping his balance as the train lurched through some dry and rocky countryside. He was trying to follow a track of winding red in the carpet when another passenger pushed him rudely out of the way without a word of excuse.

Jon looked up indignantly to find that the passenger who had jostled him aside was none other than the ragged pickpocket who had stolen the Professor's watch. He stared at the boy who was, once closely regarded, thin, sharp featured, and foreign, with dirty dark skin and ragged curls of dark hair tumbling down untrimmed about ears and neck. He wore a man's coat, overlarge on skinny shoulders, and had a hole in the knee of his trousers.

"You!" Jon exclaimed. "You stole from the Professor!"

The boy looked back at him and made a hand gesture that Jon was unfamiliar with.

"Give it back, please. The Professor is a good man."

The boy gave him an incredulous look. "Well, you're hopeful, aren't you?" he said at last, dryly, with an accent Jon could not place.

"Please," Jon tried again, stepping around in front of the boy. "I'm Jon."

"How nice for you." The boy, little taller than Jon, easily pushed him out of the way. "Now run along and play." The boy gave Jon a shove that set him off balance, and breezed down the hall to the last doors leading toward the freight cars.

"You aren't allowed to go down there!" Jon said.

The boy gave him a cool glance back over his shoulder. "And yet," he said with a wave, and opened the door. There was a sudden rush of fresh air from outside, and the boy swung himself out between the cars and began to climb nimbly up the ladder to the top of the train.

Jon stared in mingled horror and awe. He wondered if he ought to go after the boy, or go tell the Professor what had happened. He was still standing in the hall, looking at the open door, when the late light streaming in at the train window was obscured by a large dark shape. Jon looked to his right, out the window, to find it covered by a huge jet-colored wing. There was a rattling from above and down the ladder shot the pickpocket, looking pale under his layer of dirt. The boy dashed past Jon with amazing speed, and light poured in as the wing lifted again.

"Wait! Jon called. "Did you see him too?" There was no answer. The pickpocket slammed his way through the first door and on to the next, down the line of passenger cars, impossible to catch.

There were no more glimpses of either thieves or black wings that afternoon, though Jon searched hopefully through the passenger cars. He came back at last to the compartment where Tam and the Professor were now sleeping. Jon tried to take up a paper, but found himself unable to concentrate on it.

ಐ ಐ ಐ

Kara swore silently to herself as she crawled between two tall, precarious stacks of luggage and maneuvered her way on hands and knees around first a crate and then a steamer trunk.

It's too big to follow me here. I can go places it can't. If I hide it won't find me, she told herself. It wasn't fair, but Kara was used to that. Whatever she did, wherever she fled, the dark and the strange followed her. It didn't matter if she hopped a train to the far ends of the earth, the terror always followed. Things began to happen. Things went wrong, as things always went wrong, and she had to run again.

This time it was something new, a thing she had never seen before and wished now she'd never seen at all. She shivered and made herself as small as possible to squeeze between two packing cases. She grazed her knee against one sharp corner of a crate and further tore the fabric of her already ragged breeches. She bit back curses and a cry as blood, thick and dark, rose in the shallow wound. *Stupid, stupid,* she told herself.

Pulling herself out around a steamer trunk, at last she found a place to curl, in the middle of a full luggage car, in a cave formed of other people's things, hidden from view. With a few expert blows from her boot heel she broke the lock on a large trunk and pried it open, careful of the other boxes and cases piled high atop it. Inside she found clothes, and better, a soft fur coat in which to burrow.

She climbed into the trunk and set about raiding it and making a sanctuary for herself. She found a man's razor, which she pocketed for a ready weapon; a pair of breeches that were too large for her, which she pulled on right over her own and tied with a black cravat; and a pearl bracelet, carelessly tossed in a pocket of a ladies' coat. She took the bracelet but discarded the lacy pink coat with disgust.

She pulled out the pocket watch she'd nabbed off the weak scar-faced man, the one Alehd had told her to distract while he went after the real prize. Alehd was supposed to have met her on the train. He had never appeared at the meeting point. Kara tried not to think of that. It wasn't as if she liked Alehd anyway. She examined the watch, opened it. There was an inscription carved inside the cover. Kara didn't know the language, but then Kara didn't read at all. She sniffed, and put it back in her pocket.

Return it. What an absurd concept. I stole it fairly and it's mine. What a very dull little boy. Kara patted the pocket with the watch and the one with the pearl bracelet and felt a little comforted. Even if Alehd did not make it, and so could not pay her, she would have something to start over on. The only thing she lacked here was food, and she wasn't about to go venture out to the kitchen cars with a giant great *thing* waiting for her in her favorite spot on top of the train. She curled into the fur and tugged the steamer trunk shut about her hiding place. Better to stay hidden and safe and hungry.

Chapter Four
Introducing the Blackfeather Family

Jon told the Professor and Tam about seeing the pickpocket on the train but did not mention the great black wing. He didn't want the Professor to think he was telling stories, and Jon was unsure himself of just what he thought he had seen.

Tam was excited at the news about the thief. "If I see the little sneak about, I'll make him give up that watch right enough," he declared.

"Was your pocket watch terribly valuable?" Jon asked the Professor.

"I confess I don't really know," the Professor replied. "I myself treasured it. It was a gift from a good friend. But it was a thing only, not the friendship itself, and all things are transitory." The Professor touched his collar, and Jon noted than he wore something strung about his neck, under his shirt.

"I won't be able to sleep a wink," Tam grumbled. "Thieving foreigners all over the place. We should keep alert, and take turns at sleeping."

"I think we can be reasonably safe by taking the precaution of locking our compartment in the night hours," the Professor said.

Tam still insisted on staying vigilant, but the rest of the long journey passed uneventfully, without signs of thieves or any more mysteries.

The train pulled at last into their station under a blazing midday sun. The land about was hot and dry, with a few gnarled and wind-blasted trees and strange tumbled rock formations in the distance. The station stood at the center of a small sun-baked town of clay-daubed buildings and canvas awnings. Among the buildings, people went about all in foreign clothes, mostly robes and bright headscarves. Women carried large, heavy baskets on their heads, while small children ran to and fro in dirty tunics or in nothing at all.

Leaning out the compartment window, Jon smelled bad smells and good smells in the hot air, new and old aromas mingled together. Being home in Shandor smelled like clover, horses, little streams, and cool winds tumbling down from the mountains to tell one about the cedars and pines they passed. Alarna smelled like spices, strange foods, sweaty people in the hot sun, perfume, and old crumbly mud walls. It wasn't crowded like Merigvon, where the crowd never ceased, but as the train pulled in it suddenly became busy like an anthill. Carts pulled up and workmen bustled to unload one of the freight cars even as the train came to a full stop. Children crowded up around the train, calling out in languages Jon did not know, or perhaps in accents too thick for him to understand.

"Stay close to me as we disembark," the Professor said. "There should be someone waiting for us."

The hot wind hit Jon as he, Tam, and the Professor stepped off the train onto a dusty platform, and Jon had to squint his eyes against it. He gripped the Professor's hand, so as not to lose him.

"Eabrey!" the clear and pleasant voice of a woman exclaimed. "We're over here."

Jon turned, still squinting a little, to see a small greeting party waving at them from under a large green sun parasol. The woman who had addressed the Professor by his first name was very pretty and wore clothing finer and more fashionable than anything Jon's mother owned. She looked like something from the papers, with a pile of dark copper-colored hair pinned up on her head and a brimmed hat with feathers. Her face was merry and freckled and she waved an ungloved hand at them. Beside her were two children, a boy with spectacles who was only a little taller than Jon, and a small girl with a solemn face and ribbons in her long black hair.

The Professor brightened. "Hellin, how good of you to meet us." He led the boys down off the platform to stand before the lady. "Lady Blackfeather, may I introduce you to Tam and Jon Gardner, of Markerry, Shandor."

Tam nodded his head to the lady, a little awed, and Jon did the same. "Lady," he said, not sure how best to address her.

She smiled at them both. "Call me Hellin. It's lovely to meet you at last. How was your journey? Set those bags down at once. Porter! Do please put these in the carriage, thank you. This way. Would you gentleman care to stop for some refreshment before we head for the dig? We shall." Lady Blackfeather herded them all about as quickly as she had the porters, not giving them time to respond past nods and murmurs. The spectacled boy gave Jon and Tam a friendly grin. They all found themselves bundled past reaching children and loud merchants who shoved their wares forward in handfuls, into a shop across the street. Jon tumbled down into a chair beside Tam's. He found himself exchanging an awkward stare with the girl with hair ribbons across from him, before a waiter set a tall pitcher of mint water and a platter of sandwiches between them.

Across the room, the Professor guided Lady Blackfeather aside and they spoke too quietly to be heard by the children.

The boy with spectacles took the opportunity to address Jon. "You're Jon, right? I'm Djaren Blackfeather." Djaren had straight dark hair tied back in a tail like the Professor's, and green eyes, bright and eager behind his spectacles. He grinned at Jon. "I read your essay. I thought it rather brilliant. I'm so glad you've come."

Jon blinked, startled. "I, I'm glad you liked it. I didn't know Doctor Blackfeather had children."

"Well, he does, and we're them." Djaren grinned again.

A small pale hand pushed the plate of sandwiches a few inches to the left, and the serious girl with hair ribbons peered at Jon again.

"This is my sister Ellea." Djaren gestured to the little girl, who was regarding them now unblinking, with the same sober face she had kept since they first saw her. Jon found her gaze a little unsettling.

"Hello," he said. "I am pleased to make your acquaintance."

"Likewise," Ellea said, taking a sandwich.

"Hear, hear," Tam said amiably, taking four of the small sandwiches, which all fit in one of his hands. "These are funny little things. Would you like some of the water with the leaf bits?" he asked Ellea. She nodded and he helped lift and pour from the large pitcher.

Djaren pushed the sandwiches toward Jon. "Mother says your essay was best because you have a real observational eye and take the time to think things out, rather than ramming hypotheses about like runaway carts. You're mad bright, too."

"Um, thanks." Jon accepted a cup of mint water from Tam, and fished out a mint leaf with his spoon, suddenly shy.

"Djaren, dear, thank you for continuing our introductions."

Lady Blackfeather floated over in folds and ruffles of nice fabric and snagged two glasses of water and a little plate of sandwiches. "Do entertain our new guests. I am sorry, gentlemen, if I neglect you. I must have another moment with Professor Sheridan."

Tam and Jon nodded, and Lady Blackfeather excused herself and the Professor to a separate table across the shop, where she made him drink a full glass of water before they began to speak again in low voices. Jon wished he knew what they were talking about.

Tam seemed to have the same impulse. "Ten to one it's about the theft," he said.

"Theft?" asked Djaren, with interest.

Jon and Tam spoke over one another telling all about the theft in the station and the pickpocket on the train. Djaren and Ellea listened with great interest. "But what was in Uncle Eabrey's satchel?" Ellea spoke again in her careful quiet voice. "Thieves don't steal papers. They don't sparkle."

"That's a good point," Djaren agreed with his mouth full. "What were they after? It isn't as if Uncle Eabrey looks the least bit wealthy."

"He's your uncle?" Jon asked, surprised.

"More or less. Good as," Djaren explained. "Father and he grew up together like brothers, from the time they were boys. Father always sort of looks out for Uncle Eabrey, and Eabrey's always looking for clues to help with Father's cause. They've worked together for ages."

Ellea smiled oddly over the shrinking pile of sandwiches, and delicately sipped her mint water.

"He didn't seem much upset by the theft," Tam said. "He

said nothing valuable was lost."

"And that's odd, too," Djaren said, "because the only thing he ever gets really worked up about is his research, and what he's uncovered."

Jon was still keeping an eye on the grown-ups, and so he noticed when the Professor pulled the ebony feather from his breast pocket, and handed it across the table to Djaren's mother, who took it with a secret smile, and tucked it carefully into her hat.

"Well, everything seems in order," Hellin said, returning to them with the Professor at her side. "Your packages should be ready to collect and then we can be on our way. Djaren dear, do collect up the copper pieces will you? Leave a half silver."

"Of course," Djaren said amiably, sorting small coins on the tabletop. "We collect coppers," he explained to the Gardners. "You never know when you'll need a penny."

"Aren't silver more handy?" Tam asked.

"Only if you plan to spend them like money," Ellea said.

Djaren handed the last two sandwiches to Tam and Jon to pocket. "At last! Come on!" He gestured them along with him out the door and into the hot street again. "I order the papers, three of them, but they only come in once a month. Along with any books we order in. We didn't come into town last month so now I'm two months behind, and I've had nothing new to read. It's intolerable."

"We've got papers," Tam offered, keeping step beside the shorter Djaren. "The Professor got a lot of them."

"Really? Good! Then Anna and I can have at them at once. She's following some story or other in the *Times*, and I was worried we'd have a fight for the first paper."

"That story?" Tam looked a little befuddled. "Well, it doesn't end. Not as yet anyhow. The lady just faints a few more times."

"I think," Ellea said, "that she is being poisoned."

"And I *told* you," Djaren sighed, regarding his sister, "that Arienish women are *always* fainting."

"No one faints that much. She's dying, and just doesn't know it yet. All her silly troubles will be for nothing because she is going to her grave in a year. It's inevitable."

"Well, don't you go telling Anna that," Djaren said. He looked at the Gardner boys. "My sister is very cheerful, as you'll notice."

Ellea stuck out her tongue at her brother, somehow primly.

Jon exchanged a look with Tam and grinned. He was beginning to quite like the Blackfeather children. He wondered if Tam felt the same way. Tam smiled back and nodded. "It's a terrible heat, but the folk are good," he told Jon. "Mind you wear your hat."

༄ ༄ ༄

Kara watched, hot, hungry and annoyed, from under a wagon as the strange little entourage passed. The bug-eyed boy was walking beside a little princess in hair ribbons with a frock that looked like ruffles and frosting. The lout was there too, and the skinny man with all the scars, whose watch was now in her pocket. A very fancy lady was talking with him and showing them all to a dusty carriage. Mostly Kara glared at the new boy. He was particularly annoying. He could pass as easily for a girl as Kara did for a boy. Kara at once disliked the arrogant turn of his head, his long hair, fine features, and pretentious spectacles. He obviously had far too high a regard for himself.

You could tell by how he smiled all the time and never seemed to shut up.

Kara was so busy watching them that she nearly missed her chance to roll unnoticed from under the wagon before it began to lurch away. She blamed this on the heat and her now raging hunger. She swore and followed silently behind some workmen carrying trunks, hefting a heavy canvas bag of things she had collected in the baggage car. She entered the crowd at the next corner, safely anonymous, and began searching for the sign for the next meeting place. Her sharp ears caught three dialects here, but trade common seemed most prominent, which was lucky. She didn't understand the other two. She discouraged a smaller and far more amateur would-be pickpocket with a hard kick that made him curse and run off.

She was just sizing up some of the local merchants as possible fences or marks, when she found what she was supposed to be looking for. Under a faded wooden sign depicting a red pitcher she found an old man leaning by the door in the shade. She planted herself in front of him with her hands on her hips and waited for him to take notice. After a frustrating moment he finally did.

"Ah, little one. I have no coins for you. Be gone!"

"That's not what you're supposed to say." Kara gave the white-haired man a dark look. "Alehd mentioned you were a fool and half blind, but I don't find that enough of an excuse."

"What a temper the small one has," the old man muttered to himself. He squinted down at Kara, and spoke in a hushed tone. "I have seen the least and the greatest of thieves, in all kinds and all manners, but you are the smallest they have ever sent me. Don't you have some home to go to? This is no life for a little one like you. You will make your mother cry."

Kara sighed and bit back curses. She would not stab him. The daft old fool looked honestly concerned about her. *Getting old, getting soft,* Kara thought. "My last home was a packing crate," she growled. "I am tired, and I am hungry, and my mother is as dead as you are about to be if you go tell Negal that you have turned away the best lock pick in all Charesh and the five provinces of Corestemar."

The man lifted both hands, palm up. "Easy now. I do not send you away. You are welcome here, little—" he caught Kara's dangerous look, "—master lock pick." He smiled as he said it, exposing gaps of missing teeth and a hundred new wrinkles. "But where is Alehd, is he not with you?"

"He missed the train," Kara said shortly. "And he didn't pay me for my work."

"But there is work here in plenty." The old man gestured to the doorway. "Here the finest of tomb thieves have gathered in my father's time, and my father's father's. The tombs of Alarna have been my family's living. Things have changed now with the new visitors. We have now not to steal from the dead, but from other thieves."

Kara nodded slowly. "Archeologists."

"And what are they but thieves themselves? It is all the same under the sky."

"Don't flatter them," Kara said.

Chapter Five
The Discovery of the Guardians' Door

"Father's gone on business for the moment," Djaren said, opening the carriage door for his mother.

"He'll be home quite soon, I imagine." Hellin Blackfeather picked her small daughter up nimbly and set her in the carriage. Ellea bore this with dignity and chose a window seat for herself. Hellin took the hand Tam offered and climbed up into the carriage, revealing in that motion that her full skirts were in fact voluminous trousers.

The Professor followed her in. Jon wavered a moment, finding his choices were to sit between Hellin Blackfeather and the Professor, or next to Ellea, who was regarding him steadily with some unreadable expression. She edged over an inch. Jon took the motion as an invitation and sat down carefully. The Professor smiled across at him. Tam and Djaren took the remaining seats. Djaren wiped dust from his spectacles with an equally dusty handkerchief and settled them back on his nose with a smile. "Off to the dig. Wait till you see it!"

They traveled over an arid landscape on bumpy roads while Djaren described the dig and what had already been uncovered. Ellea interrupted him halfway through a description of some jeweled daggers. "The thieves took those."

Djaren looked embarrassed. "We didn't want to tell you right off," he explained, looking from Tam, to Jon, to the Professor. "No sense in alarming you, but yes, you're not the only ones to have run-ins with thieves lately."

"What else did they take?" The Professor sounded worried.

"The usual things," Djaren said.

"Everything shiny and small," Ellea answered at the same time.

"And the household silver." Hellin smiled ruefully. "I'm afraid one of the maidservants has a dangerous taste in suitors. She alone had access to the household, and she disappeared with the lot. I only hope the girl was plucky enough to get her fair share. The thieves of Alarna are not very egalitarian in their divisions."

"Mama Darvin told you not to hire her," Ellea said.

"I know, I know," Hellin Blackfeather sighed, "but I felt that girl had spirit and could make good use of some opportunity."

"Well, she did that." Djaren grinned.

"As Mama Darvin has been continually reminding me." Hellin wrinkled her freckled nose at her son.

Jon decided that Lady Blackfeather was a great deal younger than his own mother. She was extraordinarily lovely. Jon had expected something quite different. Hellin Blackfeather's name appeared as a co-author on all of Doctor Blackfeather's writings. Jon had thought she would be older, or sterner, or maybe even more like his own round, dimpled mother, whom he was trying manfully not to miss.

"Haven't you called in the authorities about the theft?" Tam asked.

"Of course," Djaren answered. "But Alarna is a small province. Thieves and authorities are close cousins here. Though up till now we've been on good terms with the lot of them."

"We've been fortunate," Hellin said. "We Shandorians are allowed to dig where others—"

"Like the Arienish," Djaren put in.

"—are not," Hellin finished.

"They take things home with them," Ellea explained. "Big things."

"One noble took home a whole temple, it's true," Djaren said. "We, on the other hand, are here for the history. Father's discoveries have founded two museums and four libraries." Djaren looked proud. "We work with governments to find and preserve treasures."

"Yes," Hellin remarked dryly. "We dig up antiquities and document them. Then the governments *sell* them to foreign nobles. Priceless artifacts for a quick penny."

"But isn't it dreadful to them to lose their history?" Jon asked, appalled.

"It would seem common sense to treasure the past, but not everyone does. Men see money for old rubbish, not a loss of valuable history."

"They forget," Ellea said gravely. "And what you forget about will come and bite you."

The carriage rumbled to a stop at last and the party tumbled out to find themselves amid a small city of bright tents, red and green and dusty yellow as well as plain canvas. It was a little like the festivals that happened back at home when the clans came down at harvest time. Except here it was hot, and oddly quiet.

"It's the time of the midday rest," Djaren explained. "The people of Alarna know there's no point working in this heat, and they know their land, so we take on Alarnan customs while we work here. Later as the air cools work will begin again and continue until the sun sets. Come see the house!"

The "house," as it turned out, was a great jumbled maze of tents, stuck one onto another in rooms and passages. Jon had once built a similar structure on a much smaller scale using sheets and his mother's kitchen chairs. The tent with the main entrance was crimson, and Djaren drew back the curtain-like doors to reveal reed mats and colorful rugs inside. A row of sandals sat in a row just inside, and the Blackfeathers began to remove their shoes.

"We guessed at sizes," Djaren explained. "I think, Tam, you'll want to wear Harl Darvin's spare set, there. He won't mind."

Tam set down the too-small pair of slippers he had been considering, and smiled in relief. "Aye, those look righter."

Jon found a pair of blue slippers that seemed to be his size exactly, and set his shoes carefully beside Tam's boots, before straightening up and looking round. Tam was already staring at their hosts' exotic looking home. There were paper lanterns and brass ones. There were low tables, high chests of drawers, and colorful pillows everywhere. Even more exciting, there were lots of bookshelves. Books and scrolls lay open on almost every available surface.

With a nod of encouragement from Hellin, Jon and Tam began to explore. Djaren followed after, grinning. "Ask me anything. I've read nearly everything in here. Mother says I'm a walking encyclopedia."

Ellea yawned. "You shouldn't brag about that."

"I wasn't." Djaren made a face at her.

She made one back.

Hellin Blackfeather clapped her hands. "Ellea, dear. Do help me find Ma Darvin, won't you?"

Ellea nodded, with a sudden little smile. "I bet she has biscuits waiting." She skipped out a doorway through a beaded curtain into a green-walled corridor.

Djaren went over to a large old steamer trunk papered with stamps and labels from all over the world, and opened it with a casual little kick. It was three quarters of the way full with copper pieces, an odd and inconvenient sort of treasure chest. Djaren tossed the new copper coins in and let the lid back down with a thump.

Tam had stopped before a glass case full of weapons. He passed over a jeweled scimitar and some graceful blades with carved ivory hilts to admire a big black Shandorian great-sword. It looked ancient indeed, pitted and chipped with age and, most likely, famous old battles. "You can tell that old sword has seen some days," Tam said, impressed.

Jon's attention, however, was drawn to the bookshelves. He

lingered over the bindings, finding several scripts and languages he didn't recognize.

"That's in Kardu," Djaren said, noting the book Jon was examining. "I'm just learning. I could teach you what I know."

Jon grinned. Despite the dust and heat, this place was beginning to look like paradise.

A short, kindly-faced woman bustled in from the green tent passage with a big copper tray. Ellea trailed her, carrying a plate of biscuits.

"I heard the carriage, Hellin dear," the woman said. "You all must be parched. Come have a drink at once. Are these the boys?"

The boys turned to be introduced to Ma Darvin. She was clearly Shandorian too, with the look of the northern clans, only rounder. She had warm brown skin, merry almond eyes, and a long black braid that wrapped around her head twice. She insisted everyone sit down amid cushions and drink sweet water with ginger before exploring any further.

Ellea solemnly deposited a biscuit in everyone's hands and then sat as well, both hands full, to nibble first one biscuit and then the other in turn, working her way in concentric circles to the center of each.

Djaren ate his biscuit normally, so Jon did too.

"Anna won't leave off with that contraption," Ma Darvin was saying. "She'd be here to greet you but just before midday the men moved the last debris from the north passage. There are some carvings she's bound and determined to record before they go on."

"Anna does the sketching," Djaren explained. "Whenever we find anything, she draws it. She's very clever at it, too."

"And she should be content with that, but no!" Ma Darvin threw her hands skyward. "Now she must drag out all the equipment and photograph it too."

"You have a camera?" Jon was impressed.

"I figured out how to work it first," Djaren said, "but Anna laid claim to it. And she *does* take better pictures. Here's one she took of us." Djaren brought down a framed photograph from an overloaded armoire dripping antiquities with labels.

Jon examined the picture with interest. There were the Blackfeathers just like in the newest kind of papers, black and white and in their best clothes. Hellin was smiling and had a fine frock. Ellea looked a little sullen in a starched dress with ribbons, and Djaren was very stiff and upright, wearing a tie. Behind them stood a tall dark figure who must be Doctor Blackfeather. There was something a little odd about his eyes.

Jon frowned and closed his own eyes a moment, trying to fix in his mind what the man looked like. He opened his eyes and studied Doctor Blackfeather's face again, but couldn't seem to hold the image in his head. The man looked striking somehow, but also just as one would expect Djaren and Ellea's father to look. Black hair, long like Djaren's, a serious face like Ellea's, and odd eyes. In another moment Jon had forgotten what the man looked like again, and had to study the picture all over. Tam, waiting impatiently for a turn, finally took it from his hands.

Next Djaren showed them their room, half green tent, half faded blue, with a cot on either side piled high with blankets and quilts. "Don't let the heat fool you," Ma Darvin said, plumping down pillows and setting thick blankets on the beds. "It can get harsh and cold here at night."

There was a writing desk, oil lamps, plenty of pens and ink and some good paper in neat stacks. Best of all, there was a bookshelf just for Jon. He carefully unpacked his own books from home onto it and felt at once more comfortable.

"And now that you're settled," Djaren said, "you must come and see the dig! If there are new carvings we have to see them. Right away!"

Back by the line of shoes, they found Professor Sheridan already waiting. "There's so much I have still to see here." He smiled. "You've uncovered so much in the last months. I've quite missed the excitement. Let's go see the new discoveries."

"I'll wait here for Corin," Hellin said. "I expect he'll be arriving shortly. You go on."

The children were back in their shoes in a matter of moments and then out into the blinding sun, Djaren carrying a jar of ginger water for Anna at Ma Darvin's insistence.

Djaren navigated the maze of tents with ease, pointing out landmarks of interest as they went. "There's the well, and the bath tents, and that's where the foreman Harl Darvin lives, with Ma Darvin and Anna. And here is the dig! Careful down the steps."

The dig opened out before them, a vast honeycomb of excavated rooms and passages, emerging roofless from the earth. It was a little like standing on a plateau and looking down into a network of canyons. Yellow sand and gray crumbling soil gave way to pale limestone and chipping red plaster. The Gardner boys duly admired the ruins.

"That must have taken a bit of work to clear," Tam said, looking at the wheelbarrows and stacks of shovels.

"Look at the drainage channels." Jon pointed. "How clever.

Bronze weapons, but they were rather advanced in other ways, weren't they?"

Djaren detailed the layout of the city under excavation, and related the order in which the buildings had been uncovered and what was in them as he guided them down into the dig itself. They descended a rope ladder and a set of wooden stairs and walked though a maze of ancient houses until they came to a thin corridor, still partially blocked with dirt. In the middle stood a large sun umbrella and a curious hooded apparatus on a tripod, under which someone in skirts was humming.

"Anna! The Professor is here, and we've brought the guests too," Djaren announced.

The apparatus and occupant jumped, with a muffled word that Jon didn't know, but that raised the Professor's eyebrows.

The tousled head of a pretty girl appeared from under the hood. "You startled me. I was taking the last exposure, but you've made me jostle it. I shall have to try again. No interrupting!" She dived back under the hood again while adjusting the apparatus. After an uncomfortable minute or two, there was a bright little explosion from a dish extending from the contraption, and the girl emerged again, looking pleased. "Done. Now introduce me at once."

"This is Anna Darvin," Djaren obeyed, "our artist and photographer."

Anna bore only a passing resemblance to her mother. She was about Tam's age, but shorter, with fine northern features and a shape more like Lady Blackfeather's than like Ma Darvin's. She had dark curly hair, tanned brown skin and startlingly blue eyes. She wore a simple, dusty blue dress with a leather apron full of pockets, paint and pencils.

Jon introduced himself, unsure whether to shake her hand or bow. He settled on a polite nod. Tam dropped his hat when Anna turned to him. He picked it up, turned it round in his hands and nearly dropped it again. "Tam," he said, with a reddening face.

Anna smiled at him. "I'm pleased to meet you, Tam Gardner."

Tam mumbled something unintelligible, and the Professor suggested they clear the way to the carving.

Anna and Djaren disassembled the apparatus and packed it away quickly, in spite of Tam's oddly clumsy efforts to assist. Anna folded down the sun umbrella and used it to wave at the revealed carvings with a flourish. "Isn't it fine? I have a good sketch of the winged fellows."

Jon peeked around the older children's backs to see the fascinating carvings. He was excited to find several different scripts and languages, and carved images. On either side of a block of script were two figures, winged men with beards.

"Guardians," Djaren said. "That's a good sign, do you see? They are only found guarding royal chambers, tombs, or treasures. There's more to be found nearby, with them here. That is, if robbers haven't already looted what they are guarding."

"I find the multiple scripts most encouraging," the Professor said, sounding breathless. "And this one, this is Sharnish. No one has ever been able to translate it. It's a dead language. No one speaks it or remembers it."

"Until now." Djaren's eyes shone. "See, there is script in four languages. Translate one and we can begin to understand all the Sharnish inscriptions in these ruins. With study—"

"—we could be the first to find out the secrets this place has been trying to show us," Anna finished, looking triumphant. "Or at least you two linguists can, and then tell us in plain trade common."

Jon pushed his way carefully to the front and examined the whole panel of carvings. He knew something suddenly, looking at it, something that had nothing to do with the languages. The edges of the panel were all obscured with chips of stone and dirt, but he knew what they would reveal. "This is a door," he said.

Chapter Six
The Return of Doctor Blackfeather

"My word, Jon, I think you are correct," the Professor said. "It's a sealed tomb passage, if I am not mistaken." The Professor pointed to a line of carved symbols. "What do you think of this?"

Jon peered up at the line the Professor indicated. "That looks almost like the writing of the Ancients, in Shandor!"

"But—" the Professor said, looking at Jon.

"It's wrong somehow," Jon said. "Less smooth, more blocky."

"As if someone who did not know it tried to copy it from another source," the Professor said.

"You're not saying it's a forgery, are you?" Djaren looked alarmed. "If someone has tampered with the dig—"

"No, I believe this to be quite as real and old as any of this place, only carved by someone inexpert in the letters. I don't think the Ancients were native to this place. This script is, like ourselves, only a visitor."

"But what does it say?" Anna asked.

The Professor, Jon, and Djaren all considered it. Djaren frowned and examined the other lines. "The Kardu section says something about a man who slew a god."

"The Alendi script says the same, I think" Jon pointed to another row of letters.

"Yes." The Professor nodded. "But the Ancient reads a little differently. While a bit unclear, this seems to be the word for warrior, not man. And nothing is mentioned about a god, only a word I think means 'a powerful evil'."

"If the scribe didn't know Ancient, how did he get even that close, though?" Djaren asked.

"It must have been what was written on the source he copied from," Jon guessed. "Someone who did speak or write Ancient must have told him what the words meant, and maybe it got garbled in translation."

"Perhaps the Ancients visited here." The Professor's eyes shone. "The original of that text might still be here, somewhere."

"Behind the door?" Anna asked.

"It looks like you could remove the stone with all the writing on it," Tam noted, "with a chisel and some ropes. Then you might be able to see in."

"But probably not," Djaren said. "We could remove the stone, but that's only set into a larger door. We've found two other broken doors so far in the excavation. If this one is like them, that stone is only a seal. There would be solid rock behind it."

"Dynamite?" Tam said.

Jon winced. "No, Tam, this is archeology. We're trying to save the past."

"Though you'd be amazed at the means early archeologists employed." The Professor shook his head. "There were a few fellows who relied heavily on dynamite. But then, they were only looking for bronze statuary, and smashed everything else underfoot."

"Barbarians," Anna sniffed.

Behind her, Tam reddened.

"Long careful hours of work will remove that door," the Professor said, "with good documentation. We'll have to try to preserve it whole. That translation stone in particular is priceless for scholarship."

"That's work for us!" Djaren grinned at Jon. "Your Alendi is better than mine. Just think, we could be the first to translate Sharnish!"

"We could be published?" Jon asked, wide-eyed. "Already? Before I'm even ten?"

"Anna has drawings published," Djaren pointed out. "It's high time we caught up."

"I want dinner." Ellea pulled at Djaren's shirt. "Not languages."

"I suppose the door isn't going anywhere," the Professor said.

Djaren threw a longing glance back at the door, but obediently picked up the camera equipment. Jon lingered another moment. Somewhere in the text, did it tell how to open the door? The ancestors of the people of Alarna couldn't have gone using dynamite or teams with ropes to open and close their doors, could they? *There must be some sort of mechanism*, Jon thought.

"Come on out of the sun, Jon." Tam took his arm. "You're turning beet red. Where did you put the hat Ma gave you?"

Jon reluctantly followed his brother out of the dig.

Walking back thought the tents in the blistering heat, Jon began to feel the sun. It was hot on his head and he felt just a little dizzy. The sand made his feet hot right through his shoes. They stopped at the Darvins' tent to leave Anna and the camera. "I'll see you at dinner." She smiled. "Mama will want help and I have to wash the dust from my hair."

Jon tripped once on uneven hillocks of sand and the

Professor looked at him with concern. "Let's get you in the shade."

They reached the Blackfeathers' sprawl of connected tents and Jon and Ellea went in first to take off their shoes. Coming out of the sun into shade, Jon's dazzled eyes kept seeing things that weren't there. He was pushing off his last shoe when Ellea suddenly bolted across the room with a happy cry. "Poppa!"

Jon turned a little too quickly, to see only a confusion of burning green fires and streamers of black cloth, hair, and feathers on an unseen wind. For a moment he thought he saw again the strange and inhumanly beautiful man's face from the train station, but then in a startled blink it was all gone. There was not a maelstrom of blackness and green fire, just the sitting room. Hellin sat in an armchair, and in the center of the room stood a tall man in flowing black robes who was even now picking up and spinning Ellea with a weightless grace. She shrieked with laughter.

Doctor Blackfeather was as confusing in real life, Jon thought, as he was in the photograph. Something about him would not stick in Jon's mind. There was some resemblance between the children and their father, Jon saw, but he could not quite remember what it was. He thought Doctor Blackfeather looked young, but then he instantly wondered if he was in fact quite old. He frowned and blinked again, feeling stupid for being affected by the heat like this.

"You're home!" Djaren also pelted across the room and stood before his father, grinning.

The Professor, now in house sandals, smiled warmly at Doctor Blackfeather. "Corin, it is so good to see you!"

Looking again at Doctor Blackfeather, Jon's vision at last

cleared. The Doctor's eyes were jet black, as were his clothes, in an exotic mix of native and gentleman. He wore flowing robes like the men of Alarna, but underneath those his clothes were a more elegant, severe, and up to date version of the Professor's. He seemed to wear a lot of layers and not mind the heat.

Doctor Blackfeather greeted the Professor with a warm handshake, and Jon could see them both quite distinctly. Doctor Blackfeather was taller than the Professor by quite a bit, with an oddly ageless face that seemed at once familiar and strange. His long black hair and robes moved almost weightlessly as he set Ellea down on a chair, and then settled himself on some floor pillows, northern style. Even sitting, he was tall.

Perhaps, Jon considered, Doctor Blackfeather was originally from one of the very far northern clans of Shandor. He might be from one of those mysterious places still half cloaked in mist and old folk stories about sea birds that talked in riddles, and creatures in the dark pines who could take on many shapes long, long ago. He might be from clan White Gull maybe, or New Starfire. Doctor Blackfeather felt like a story Jon had heard once and forgotten.

The Professor and Djaren were both excitedly speaking of the new discovery, and Doctor Blackfeather had not yet said a word, but he smiled, and the smile reminded Jon of one Tam gave him sometimes.

Hellin stood and came over to take a hard look at Jon. "Let's get you some water. Come have a seat. There's a nice breeze from the shady north that will do you good." Jon allowed himself to be led over to the armchair and settled into it with a cool cup of water and a damp towel round his neck. Tam, protesting, was given the same treatment and installed on an adjoining divan. Jon grinned at his brother, noting his fine sunburn.

"Don't you boys have hats?" Hellin asked them.

"I dropped mine, I think," Tam apologized.

Doctor Blackfeather shifted to finish the circle in which they were now sitting, and nodded at each of the brothers in turn. "Jon, Tam, it is good to meet you at last. I am sorry I was unable to welcome you at the station." The Doctor's voice was low and soft, with a Shandorian accent as thick as Tam's. Jon felt more comfortable at once. He wasn't sure what kind of voice or words he'd been expecting. Nothing so warmly human, he thought. The Doctor might have sounded like the sea, or wind through canyon walls, or like falling water. Ellea claimed a place in the Doctor's lap, Djaren took a seat beside him, and the Doctor transformed into an ordinary father.

"I had notes for you," Professor Sheridan said, "I'll need to reconstruct them. I'd half forgotten, what with seeing the new texts here."

"I have good news for you about that, Eabrey," the Doctor said. He reached into his robes and brought out, as if by magic, the Professor's satchel.

"The authorities recovered it," Tam said. "Well, that's some good come of that mess. Did they find the pickpocket too?"

Doctor Blackfeather frowned, while Professor Sheridan eagerly took back his satchel and began to pull sheaves of notes from it. "What else was stolen?" Doctor Blackfeather asked.

"Only a pocket watch." The Professor waved dismissively. "These are what I have missed. My notes! Thank you, Corin. Thank you very much. I was dearly missing these. I did hope . . . and you did. Thank you."

"I should have traveled the whole way with you," Doctor Blackfeather said.

"It's really all right, Corin," the Professor assured.

Jon shifted in his seat so that his feet could touch the floor, and in moving found something stuck between the cushions. It was a large dark feather. He looked at the Doctor.

Doctor Blackfeather watched him back. "I am glad to have you here, Jon Gardner. Your essay was very well thought out, and shows you to be remarkably observant."

"Thank you, sir," said Jon.

"To see things clearly is a great gift," the Doctor said, holding Jon's gaze in his own. His eyes were not completely black after all. There was green in them, deep and burning.

"He really is observant," Djaren said. "He saw right away that the carvings were part of a door. He's going to help with the translations."

"I think he will be a great help here," Professor Sheridan added. "He has an eye for detail and a head for mysteries."

"Well, next time you are all out deciphering mysteries in carvings you will kindly remember to use a sunshade and wear hats," Hellin said. "Now, dinner won't wait, and you can't all sit down covered in dust and old bones. Go get cleaned up."

They all trooped out obediently, leaving the Doctor and Hellin Blackfeather alone in the sitting room. Jon heard them speaking together in hushed voices as he left the room but could not make out the words. Hellin had moved from her chair to sit close to her husband and they leaned in to each other, his hand lifting to touch her copper hair. With a twinge of homesickness Jon missed his own parents. He straightened up resolutely and followed Tam to their room. This summer was going to be exciting. There was no time to be small or homesick; he was going to be a scholar now, and maybe even published. That thought alone made him dizzier than the sun had.

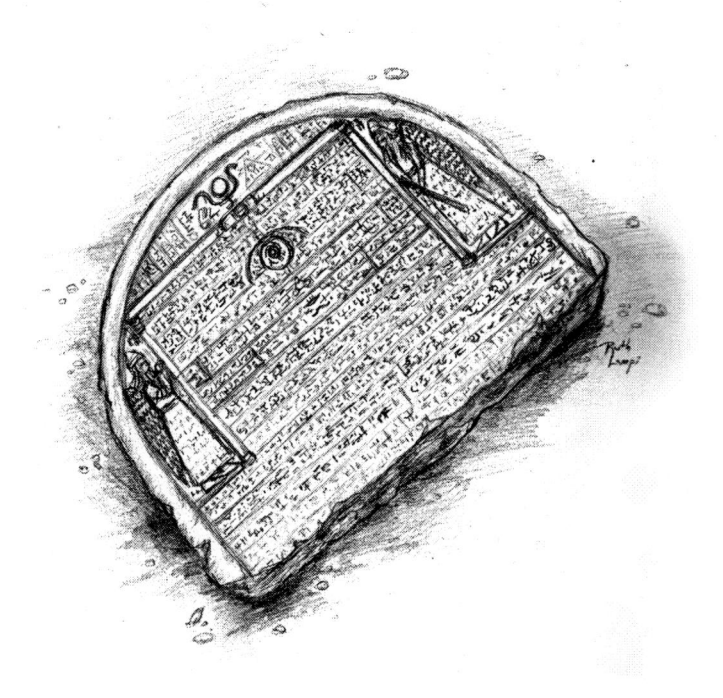

Chapter Seven
Thieves in the Night

Hellin looked in on Jon later after he and Tam had washed up and dressed. She insisted on re-applying wet towels to Jon's head and neck, and giving them both a salve for sunburn. "You'll soon be healthy and brown as Alarnans, but southern Shandorian skin takes a while to acclimate." She smiled. "Put this cream on every morning and every night, and any time it starts to sting. And wear your hats. How are you feeling, Jon?"

"Quite better now," Jon said, truthfully.

"Good," Hellin said. "Then let us see about dinner."

Dinner proved to be a splendid and crowded affair, and not nearly so formal as Jon had imagined it would be. Ma Darvin was nearly as good a cook as Jon's own mother. She, Anna, and Anna's father Harl the quartermaster shared the same long table as the Blackfeathers and their guests. There was a great deal of excited discussion about translations, and digging, and the best way to move a large door. Harl, a big man with a heavy northern accent whose idea of dressing for dinner was wearing a clean shirt rolled up to the elbows, offered the help of his work teams that very evening.

"Let us study it where it is first," the Professor said. "We need to find out more about it, and how it is settled in the passage."

"I want another look at that corridor too, before Anna scampers back into it," Harl said. "I want to make sure that passage is sound and won't come tumbling down. I'd like to shore up those walls with some planks."

"And we might cover the area with tarps as well, so dust

won't gather on what we've cleaned," Anna said.

"The shade won't hurt either," Hellin said. "And it's my turn to admire the carvings."

഼   ഼   ഼

After a long, hot, but happy evening of brushing sand from carvings, grubbing for interesting bits of debris on the passage floor, and squinting over translations in a crowded corridor, Jon was all too happy to be able to collapse into his new bed. Everyone had been able to take turns visiting the bathing tents. Now Jon lay on soft quilts, clean, covered in sunburn salve, and happy. He fell asleep quickly.

Jon was not sure what it was that woke him. He found himself suddenly sitting up wide awake in bed, his heart pounding. He heard a noise then, not close, but from somewhere outside, at a distance. It was a grinding noise, followed by a thud. In the next bed, Tam stirred. Jon climbed quickly out of bed and grabbed his brother's shoulder.

"Tam, Tam, there's something out there!"

Tam rolled over and grunted. He rubbed his eyes and struggled his way out of his sheets. "Where?"

Jon pulled at Tam's arm and dragged his sleepy brother toward the tent flap that led outside. He ducked under and pulled Tam after. The moon was nearly invisible, just a tiny sliver in the sky, and it was quite dark. Jon and Tam threaded their way quietly among the tents, out to the edge of the dig where Jon paused, shivering. Tam frowned and rubbed his eyes again. "The workmen don't come out here to dig in the middle on the night."

There was rustling somewhere below, and whispered voices. Tam went down the rope ladder, keeping Jon behind him, and they carefully rounded a few corners. When they came closer to the corridor with the carvings, Tam stopped, and Jon peered around him to see the quick glimmer of a hooded lantern and the shadowy shapes of robed figures.

"Oi!" Tam shouted, in the deepest voice he could muster. "What's this?"

The figures jumped and scattered, running in all directions. A familiar small shape rushed past Jon, pushing him hard out of the way with a bony elbow.

"Thieves!" Tam bellowed. "Wake up and catch them!"

Sounds from the camp above told them that others were awake now. Jon darted forward into the now empty carvings corridor and Tam ran in after him. Someone had dropped the lantern, but it was still burning. Jon lifted the shutter, held the lantern high, and looked about. There were ropes, chisels, and footprints on the ground, and the big carved door had a blank missing segment. Behind the missing tablet was only bare rock. The thieves had stolen the translation stone.

༄ ༄ ༄

The children gathered in the sitting room wrapped in quilts while the adults had a quiet conversation down the hall in the Doctor's study.

"I don't understand, why would they take the stone?" Jon said. He sat on the divan beside Tam, sipping tea that Ma Darvin had distributed to "calm the nerves."

"It isn't shiny," Ellea agreed, from her spot amid floor pillows.

"But it would be priceless to a scholar," Djaren said, his voice hushed, "or to a rival archeologist. Father has made some enemies over the years." He wasn't wearing his spectacles, and he looked a bit like his father.

"They would have to be close though, to know about what we found so quickly," Anna pointed out. She was wrapped in a dressing gown and a quilt, and had taken over Hellin's armchair.

"I haven't seen any familiar faces," Djaren admitted.

"But I have. Sort of." Jon explained about the small figure who had pushed past him.

"What kind of thieves steal a satchel full of notes and then a translation stone?" Tam asked.

"They have to be working for some employer," Djaren insisted. "We should start looking for people who don't belong in Alarna. We should go into town and make inquiries."

"If that pickpocket followed you all the way from the grand terminal, he certainly can't belong here," Anna said.

"We're dealing with outsiders then," Djaren agreed. "If we identify them, maybe we can find out who they are working for."

"I want some words with that little thief," Tam said.

"He still has the Professor's pocket watch," Jon said. "Unless he's sold it."

"That could be hard, in Alarna," Djaren said. "Gems, gold and statues you can pawn here, through the so-called antiques dealers, but not pocket watches."

"Djaren tried to pawn one he got for a birthday," Ellea added.

Djaren glared at her. "I think that someone was denied permission to dig here, and is trying to steal what we've found. The Arienish and the Levour have asked for permission to excavate here and have been refused. Remember last year at Mervoe, when Chauncellor tried to bribe our workers?"

Anna nodded.

"I think," Djaren said, "that one of father's old enemies is back and trying to make trouble for us."

"And with the stone lost, how will we ever translate the Sharnish?" Jon asked the most painful question.

Djaren looked sick. "They stole our research." He reached up to adjust his spectacles and, not finding them, frowned.

"You're forgetting," Anna said, with a wicked smile, "that it's not so lost as that. I took photographs, remember, and the thieves didn't get those. The camera is safe under my bed."

"Can we develop them at once?" Djaren leapt to his feet.

"No, I need more supplies. There's a package coming for me by mule caravan up from Sheblas with more silver nitrate. It might have arrived at the depot in town by tomorrow if we're lucky. With that I can set up my dark room and get started."

Tam nodded. "So we get your tools or whatnot in town and see if we can't find some thieves to question."

"Or some unscrupulous thieving archeologists skulking in the hotel," Djaren said. "Be on the look out for anyone too pale or too well dressed for this place."

Jon considered Doctor Blackfeather's appearance and decided that he certainly fit that description, but he didn't say anything. He was nervous and excited about what the next day would bring.

It was hard to fall back asleep that night, but at last Jon did, despite Tam's snores.

Chapter Eight
What Amazing Events Can Transpire in Half an Hour

The next day all the children had excuses for why they wanted to go into town. Hellin regarded them at breakfast with an amused but cynical eye. "If I didn't know better, I'd think you were all plotting something."

Jon reddened and looked down at his plate.

Djaren adjusted his spectacles and gave his mother a grin. "Did Father and Uncle Eabrey have breakfast early? They aren't here. Are they investigating?"

Hellin looked at her son with her chin cupped in one hand. Djaren blinked back at her, sitting up straight. "Very well, I will take you with me." Hellin said. "I have some errands to run, myself. And as Corin and Eabrey have business elsewhere, I'd rather have you with me than off plotting on your own."

"Thank you, mother."

"Thank you, Lady Blackfeather."

Hellin sighed. "The carriage will be waiting. Come on."

ಌ ಌ ಌ

The village was no less hot or dusty than it had been on the day of their arrival, only yesterday. The smells were just as strange and exciting, and in the morning the village was busy. A caravan blocked up the thin twisting streets, so they left the carriage at the edge of town with the driver, a local man with a red turban and what Jon thought was the funny name of Hezdri.

Hellin guided them expertly through the warren of dirty streets, around donkeys and camels, and past nomads in brightly colored layers of robes and tunics. People carried baskets and rolls of cloth in and out of shops. Women sold things laid out on blankets or piled up in open baskets. There were many kinds of foods Jon had never seen or smelled before, and clothes and tools with no clear purpose that he could understand. People seemed to want them though, as they stood crowding the streets and yelling about the things on blankets. Jon thought that bartering, as Djaren called it, sounded rather a lot like shouting. Market day seemed a lot louder and more exciting here than it did back home in Markerry.

Hellin led them past the market and the small groups of grubby children and beggars asking for coins. They stopped before the tea shop they had visited yesterday.

"All those nomads are the Dashmadi," Djaren explained. "They're from the hill country and they live in tents. We asked some of them to help with the dig, but their people don't believe in archeology. They say that the ruins belong to the dead, and that what belongs to the dead is forbidden to touch."

"Though they seem quite practical about it," Hellin said, rummaging through her bag. "The Dashmadi believe that only the bad things about the departed stay with their remains, and that all that was light and good and free about them ascends into cloud, and that the best of what came before watches with the cloud, and blesses the people with rain. It's a lovely way to think about it."

Ellea scratched her nose. "They think graves are haunted by demons made of the baddest bits of people, and if you steal from a grave or touch a corpse you'll be cursed, and end up belonging to the dead too."

"You may see why the Dashmadi don't always get along with

the Alarnans," Djaren said.

"With all the tomb robbing and so on," Ellea said.

"Not something to be discussed in public," Hellin warned. "We're guests here and should be civil. You can all go with Anna and get that package from the depot. I have some errands to run. I want to see you all back here in half an hour. I trust you can stay out of trouble for that long at least and refrain from accusing the locals of theft."

"We'll be polite, Ma'am," Jon said.

"I know you will, dear." Hellin smiled and ruffled his hair.

"We know our way around the village," Djaren said.

"That's what I'm afraid of." Hellin patted Jon's shoulder, gave a small bag of coins to Anna, and set off down the street.

"She's wearing one of her best dresses, and she's heading for the hotel. I'll bet mother is on the lookout for the rival archeologists and other mysterious foreigners. She can talk information out of anybody." Djaren grinned. "That leaves finding the thieves to us."

"But do let's get my packages first," Anna insisted. "My fingers are itching to get that film developed."

Djaren agreed, and they headed for the depot.

Tam looked about at the merchants as they went, pulling Jon out of the way of a camel at one crowded intersection. "The Dash people seem to take better care of their livestock anyway," he observed. "That camel looked better off than some of the little begging fellows." He looked at Anna. "Are the nomads like our K'shay tanna back home at all?"

Anna laughed. "Well, they don't build, and only live in cloth or leather homes that can be taken down and carried, but that's about it."

"Well, and both cultures have long traditions of warriors and sword fighting, and places one can bring one's sword," Djaren said. "And swords all have names and sometimes get introductions at the door."

"But that's just normal, really." Anna shrugged. "Isn't it? But it's better to be a girl in the K'shay tanna. At thirteen, we get a knife, but Dashmadi girls just get another scarf they have to wear around their heads. A knife is a lot more useful, I think."

"I've seen you use yours to mix up paints," Djaren said.

"Hush, you. Don't you ever let my mother know. I'd get a lecture. And here's the depot."

The depot was a dusty low building that seemed quite crowded, so Anna went in with just Tam to help elbow through, and the others waited outside. Anna's package had come, and she stowed it carefully in a large handbag, along with the coin purse Hellin had given them. The children moved out of the crowds and gathered in an alleyway to discuss their plans.

"We need to find out where the thieves might be hiding," Tam said to Djaren. "You and I could go look for them. Anna can watch the little ones in the tea shop."

"Excuse me!" Anna said indignantly.

"Please, size is hardly an indicator of facility." Ellea regarded Tam coldly.

Djaren winced. "We're all safer as a group, really. And you don't want Anna or Ellea mad at you. Knives, remember? Besides, I have an idea of where to start looking. You said the pickpocket had Uncle Eabrey's watch. We should try the worst of the antique dealers."

They went first to the shop where, Djaren informed them,

blushing, he had attempted to pawn the unwanted pocket watch.

"There were flowers on it," he explained. "Pink."

Tam nodded sympathetically.

Anna laughed. "Boys can be entirely irrational."

The ramshackle shop was as dingy inside as out, with piles of objects heaped everywhere from floor to ceiling. It looked as if some of the stacks were actually supporting the roof. Some of the objects might have been very valuable, but a lot of it looked to Jon like rubbish. He only glanced at the antiques for a moment. A familiar ragged figure stood at the counter having a loud argument with the proprietor, who was easily five times his size, mostly in girth. Djaren had been entirely right in his choice of places likely to house thieves. Jon tugged at Tam's sleeve and pointed excitedly.

"Three silver? What do you think I am? Those are real pearls, and worth more than half this miserable pile of refuse you call a shop!" The pickpocket was berating the shopkeeper.

"You must be mistaken." The man spread his fat hands. "They are small pearls, probably paste. I am generous to offer you even so much, but I have a heart for small children."

The pickpocket answered with something unbelievably rude.

The shopkeeper looked up then and saw the newcomers. His hand closed over the pearls on the counter, hiding them from view. "Ah! Little master, are you here to buy a gift, perhaps for your small sister?" He addressed Djaren, rising from his seat with difficulty and speaking in oily tones.

The pickpocket turned too, annoyed, and stared at them.

"You deal with thieves. I should report you," Djaren drew himself up to his full height, still considerably less than Tam's, and frowned.

"No, no, not at all," the shopkeeper protested. "This boy, he tries to sell me stolen property, and I send him away. Get out!" he yelled at the pick pocket, and made as if to strike him.

The boy dodged the blow easily, looking angry. "Pig son of a diseased goat! You have my pearls in your filthy hands, and you will give them back!"

"I have nothing to do with thieves! Get out or I will beat you!" the man cried.

The pickpocket cursed bitterly and rounded on the children, cornered. Jon stepped back. He had never seen anyone look so furious.

"You stole the Professor's pocket watch." Tam said to the boy.

"You know who stole the stone at the dig," Djaren added, "and you're going to tell us."

The pickpocket snarled at them. "You are really starting to annoy me. I've been having a bad day. Don't make me spoil yours."

"But you *did*," Jon spoke up. "Your friends stole our research. We just want it back. Please." He met the pickpocket's angry black eyes.

"You're really a hopeful child, aren't you?" The pickpocket met his eyes and smiled bitterly. "The world isn't nice. Get used to it." He wheeled on the shop keeper. "I won't forget you. And I promise you won't forget me."

The boy vaulted over a pile of trash with amazing speed and darted between Tam and Anna. He kicked at a spot behind Tam's right knee, sending him sprawling, and wrenched away Anna's handbag with a deft motion. The boy then eluded an interception attempt by Djaren and leapt onto the counter.

"You ruin my day, I ruin yours." The boy sprang off the counter toward the back entrance.

"Look after Ellea! Tea shop!" Djaren told Anna, and raced promptly after the pickpocket. The pickpocket swung a quick turn about a support beam, and kicked a heavy statue into the next beam. The beam cracked and swayed.

"Get out! Everybody!" Tam yelled. He picked up Ellea with one arm, grabbed Jon with the other, and plunged out the front door with Anna at his heels as the whole structure began to give. The pickpocket and Djaren raced off right through the falling building's back entrance into a maze of alleyways. The fat shopkeeper barely made it out as the whole place tumbled down in billows of dust. He stood coughing and quivering with fury, one sweaty hand gripping the pearl bracelet.

"Tea shop," Anna said breathlessly, taking Ellea from Tam. "Come on, we have to be ready!"

"For what?" Tam asked, pulling a very startled Jon along after him.

Jon looked back at the swearing shopkeeper for a moment, and tried to see where Djaren and the pickpocket had gone. In the swirling dust there was no sign of either of them.

Chapter Nine
A Rooftop Chase and a Grim Revelation

Kara dashed around one corner and another, cursing her terrible luck. The boy behind her was not losing ground. His nice clothes were dust covered and his hair was coming loose, but he was not giving up. Kara was beginning to suspect he knew these alleyways. She didn't, not yet. This place was still new. But no bespectacled little pretty-boy was going to catch her when she wanted to disappear. She found a set of uneven steps around another corner, and dashed up them to the roof tops. The boy followed. Kara ran along above the narrow streets, upsetting birds, and hopping up and down levels as they changed. The boy stayed right behind her.

Kara growled. Time to shake him up a bit. She leapt a narrow alleyway across to another network of roofing. He made the jump. She took a riskier one. He did too. She looked back. He was grinning.

That was it. Kara jumped headlong off the next rooftop, rolled down an awning and landed just right, with her knees bent, in a crowded street below. She began to weave through the crowd, looking back. No sign of him on the rooftop. She grinned and hefted the handbag. It had a good weight. She wondered what the pretty girl had in it. A nice jingle of coins came from somewhere in the depths. A small, dirty urchin lifted a hand beseechingly, hearing the coins. Kara frowned. "Steal your own," she told the child.

Everyone wanted something for nothing. Kara looked for landmarks, scanning the colored shop signs and searching for the wells that marked certain squares. There was one ahead, and there was the annoying boy with spectacles. He had taken them off and was scanning the crowd with sharp green eyes. He looked a little the worse for wear. His long hair was loose and tangled and he now had a skinned knee, but he seemed quite cheerful. To Kara's surprise and horror, he spotted her. He moved to one corner of the square, and she darted off to the other.

The chase started again, this time through busy streets. Kara wove in and about the crowd, shoving people out of the way when necessary. To her great annoyance, the boy did not lose ground. He dodged people rather well. It was time for a different tactic. Kara took to the less crowded alleyways again.

Sometimes you had to convince people to stop following you the hard way. Kara crouched down behind a rain barrel after rounding a corner into a convenient alley. The boy dashed by but began to slow, not seeing her. She put her foot out as he was passing her hiding place and tripped him. He went sprawling, but intelligently, rolling with his fall. Kara sprang at him before he could regain his feet. She got in a good blow that bloodied his nose, but then he set her off balance and they went rolling in the dust, fists flying. Kara got the upper hand by kicking him in the shin. She grabbed about as they careened past a rubbish heap and found something solid to hit with. After a scuffle for it, which was dangerously close, Kara came out on top. She sat on the boy, holding her weapon, a large, empty glass bottle.

"If you don't stop following me, I'm going to break both your glasses and your face," she informed the boy.

He looked up at her, wide-eyed. "I believe you." Then he grinned. Kara was taken aback. Someone grabbed her arms from behind, taking the bottle from her grasp and pulling her up bodily into the air.

"Mind his feet, Tam! He kicks hard," the boy on the ground called.

Kara found herself hauled around by the collar and held up against the alley wall helpless and kicking, by none other than the lout boy. The two girls in their pretty frocks and the little bug-eyed boy were looking on. From somewhere nearby Kara could smell the aroma of tea. She swore. She'd been tricked. The smug little boy in spectacles had driven her right into a trap. She swore at him explosively, feet dangling.

He picked himself up off the ground and touched his bloody nose gingerly. He looked up at her in surprise. "You know Kardu?"

The older girl, the new one in lace and blue ribbons, ran to the injured boy's side with a worried cry. Kara hated her immediately.

"Djaren, you look terrible! Did he hurt you badly?"

"I'm all right, Anna, thank you. There's your bag." Djaren pointed proudly.

Kara swore at him some more.

Djaren stared at her, amazed. "And Alendi? We have to talk."

The big boy had some trouble restraining Kara as the pretty girl retrieved her bag from where it had fallen and brushed it off officiously. The girl looked inside, and the other one, tiny princess hair ribbons, came over to look too.

"Look here, you're a bad sort," the lout informed her. "But

now you're fair caught, and we want some answers."

"I don't speak idiot," she told him.

The lout's face reddened several shades, and a vein appeared on his neck.

"Don't let him rattle you, Tam," Djaren advised, taking the handkerchief the older girl offered, and clamping it to his bleeding nose.

"You have minions, good for you," Kara told Djaren, trying to kick Tam the lout boy. He tightened his grip on her collar. "Five to one is sporting, isn't it? You must be *nobility*." She gave the word an acid edge.

"There's no nobles in Shandor," Tam said, angry. "And you weren't fighting fair."

"You like playing the man when the girls are watching, don't you?" Kara hissed at Tam. "They don't much notice you otherwise, do they?"

His face turned redder. Kara grinned at him. Get him mad enough and he would let go with one hand to hit her. That was all she'd need to escape. She'd kick him in the—

A new voice interrupted the proceedings, a woman's voice. "And just what are you all doing? Can't I leave you safe for half an hour? Put the little girl down at once!"

"Mother, he stole," Djaren began.

"Girl?" Tam asked, blanching.

"Lady Blackfeather, this is the pick pocket!" the bug-eyed boy sang out.

The tall and finely dressed lady with amazing copper hair advanced on them and took charge of the situation at once. "That's a little girl, yes, Tam. Don't let her go, but please don't shake her so. She may have an awful mouth, but she's half starved and in a bad state."

"Ma'am, I never meant—" Tam's grip weakened, and he looked with horror from the lady to the pretty girl in blue ribbons. Kara took the opportunity to try and kick him, but Djaren intervened, and grabbed her legs. "Sorry," he mumbled. "But Tam, be careful. Girl or not, she's mean."

The tiny girl stepped up to glare at Kara. "I am not princess hair ribbons," she declared. Kara frowned. She did not remember speaking those words.

The little girl sniffed, and went to go hold the lady's hand.

Kara struggled uselessly, held by the two boys. She swore at them with the worst words she knew. They did not appear to comprehend them. The lady, however, did.

"Interesting," she said. "I think we'd better take her back with us. She could use a good meal. Are you from Corestemar, dear?"

Kara spat at her.

"Yes, I thought so." The lady smiled. "Djaren, dear, you look a mess. I don't even want to know how you captured her. Is your nose all right?"

"Yes, Mother."

"Then if you have quite finished getting into trouble here, I suggest we go home."

"Yes, Mother." Djaren grinned around the handkerchief.

"You can't kidnap me. You'll be sorry. I have friends," Kara snapped at them.

The lady gave Kara a very insulting look of sympathy. "You don't lie very well yet, dear. You do better with threats. We don't mean you harm, but I think you should have a talk with Doctor Blackfeather."

"You can't make me talk," Kara growled.

Djaren coughed.

Kara attempted to kick him.

"We may need a second carriage," the lady said. "Anna, can you see to that?"

"Certainly, Lady Blackfeather." The pretty girl nodded.

Kara found herself stuffed, not un-gently, into a carriage with the lady and Djaren. She had been bound carefully with belts and hair ribbons. She mocked her captors throughout the process, but accepted the mint water the lady gave her before they tied her hands. The others were in the next carriage and out of kicking range. Kara found Djaren and the lady a bit harder to anger. The boy kept asking her questions like "Can you pick locks?" and "Can you teach me?" and the lady didn't ask her anything at all, which was more unnerving. Kara had thought of a hundred escape plans by the time they reached the dig site, but decided not to try them just yet. She was determined not to come away from this empty handed. If they were going to drag her home, she was going to take a bit of that home back with her. Archeologists had valuable things. And then she would go get that bracelet back.

ஐ   ஐ   ஐ

Lady Blackfeather had workmen assist in installing Kara in a small shed with a cot, a basin of wash water, and an impressively huge meal. Lady Blackfeather did not let any of the other children in, but sat herself with Kara for a little while. Kara had the strong feeling that she should not try anything with Lady Blackfeather. There was something about her that said she had strength beyond the obvious six workmen outside.

"Did you drug the food? You seem to really want me to eat

it," Kara said, sniffing at the dinner items. She glared at Lady Blackfeather.

"You've had a bad life, I take it," Lady Blackfeather said, looking regretful. "I promise we have not altered the food. I know that's not enough, but do believe that we want you conscious and answering some questions later this evening. And perhaps cleaner than you are now."

Kara snorted.

Lady Blackfeather brought out a bundle of clean clothing. "Djaren outgrew these last year. You could use some things in your own size. I also noted that when you were kicking, your boot soles were coming off. If you will refrain from using these on my children, I give them to you." The lady held out a pair of sturdy black work boots.

"Are you trying to bribe me?" Kara asked.

"No, dear, to mother you. It's a bad habit, I know, but I can't help it." Lady Blackfeather smiled. "I have a soft spot for tortured and lonely souls. And plucky children. You deserve better than this."

She brushed an old bruise on Kara's face and Kara flinched back, ready to lash out.

"You don't have to go back to them," Lady Blackfeather said.

"Don't waste your pity. I'm not impressed," Kara growled. "Go feed a kitten or something and leave me alone."

Lady Blackfeather sighed. "The offer still stands. Make what you will of it. Doctor Blackfeather will see you later, when he returns."

Kara did not like the sound of that. She distrusted doctors immensely. As soon as Lady Blackfeather left she sniffed at the food and, finding no suspicious odors, she devoured as much of it as she could. The rest she stuffed into the pillow case. She splashed a little of the wash water on her face and neck to keep cool, and drank some more of it.

She did get into the new clothes and boots, and found them to her liking. They were in dark colors, good and sturdy, with a little repair work here and there. Both knees of the trousers had carefully sewn patches. She kept her big coat and filled the pockets with leftovers and some of the nicer dishes. There was no silver, unfortunately, only wooden utensils. Kara took them anyway, and began using them to dig at the rear corner of the shed.

Through cracks between boards, she noted where the workmen were watching. She waited patiently and kept digging, and was rewarded by seeing them move a little further off into the shade as the sun progressed across the sky. One of them at last dozed off, and it was time. Kara wriggled through the hole she'd made in the corner, and emerged silent and dirt covered behind the shed, near the sleeping workman. She dragged the pillow case of food out after her and crept through the camp to where the carriage horses were picketed. She untethered one and climbed up onto its back. She would come back to steal something later, but now she was already late. Her contacts would be meeting their employers tonight and handing over the rock they had stolen. Kara raced off on horseback, into gathering twilight.

It was fully night when she reached the meeting place. Torchlight flickered in the darkness ahead. She climbed off the horse, sent it on its way with a slap, and crept up to the rendezvous, a hollow amid old ruins, silent and listening. There were voices. She recognized Negal's voice and that of the old man Himar. They sounded nervous. A bad smell hung in the air, acrid and rotting. Kara moved closer, still silent. She peered out between two stones and saw a group of figures in the firelight. A tall, robed man with an unfamiliar voice spoke. The voice was hoarse, wet, and rasping. The accent reminded Kara of the place she'd come from, of slums in the shadows of great crumbling temples, of crowds and crying children, and people with nothing left to steal living beside palaces. That accent belonged to past and nightmares, not here.

"You have brought it here?"

"Yes, lord," Negal said, "and we want our payment." Negal stood with his band of a dozen thieves, facing a group of twenty men in dark, hooded robes. The stolen stone sat upon the ground between them.

"And what," the large man with the terrible voice asked, "do you think the worth of a rock is?"

"You promised, lord, to reward us well. You *asked* for this stone."

"I did." His voice cut off, followed by a sniffing sound. His hooded head moved from side to side and turned in Kara's direction. "Something watches," the voice said. "Someone is here."

"We were unfollowed," old Himar said. "We never betray a bargain. We are honest thieves."

"What a term." The horrible voice made a wheezing sound Kara realized was laughter. The smell grew stronger as the hooded figure began to move toward Kara's hiding place. She froze, staring. One hand emerged from the figure's robe, visible in the torchlight. It was the arm of a rotting corpse.

"Lord!" Negal gasped.

Kara was about to run, but was interrupted by a sudden rush of wind as something huge swooped down low overhead. The thieves did not seem to notice, but the robed stranger did. He hissed in fury. "The sky! He is here! Fire!"

All the robed figures brought out things from under their robes—rifles. The thieves fled as the robed men began firing wildly into the black sky. It was deafening. The corpse man brought out a rifle as well and used it with a more studied aim. Kara caught a glimpse of one milky white eye. She clapped both hands over her ears and ran, along with the other thieves, for cover, for safety. A muffled gasp came from above, and something wet fell on her hand. She squinted at it and saw black droplets. She ran faster, losing herself in the night.

Chapter Ten
A Marvelous Secret Revealed

Jon was having trouble sleeping again. A lantern lit the sitting room, where Hellin's shadow was visible as she sat waiting up for Doctor Blackfeather to return. Jon could see her silhouette clearly though his tent wall as she picked up a book, set it down again, poured a cup of tea and then let it sit, ignored. She was worried. That worried Jon, too.

The children had spent all afternoon getting in Anna's way as she tried to set up the dark room and develop the photographs. The pictures were drying now in a little line, carefully left alone to work their magic now that Anna had done with them. The children had spent another part of the evening in a fruitless search for the missing pickpocket girl. When the Professor had come back in the late afternoon they had all told him breathlessly about their day. And then Doctor Blackfeather had not returned, and continued not to return. Hellin had insisted they all get some sleep, and now she waited alone in the sitting room, sometimes sitting, sometimes pacing. Jon watched her, sleepless.

The whinny of a horse came from outside, and Jon saw Hellin's face turn to the tent's entrance. She put a hand to her lips as a strangely shaped shadow lurched into view. The shadowy mass unfolded into several more unrecognizable silhouettes before falling into her outstretched arms, in more recognizable dimensions. Jon held his breath. He could just barely hear their whispers.

"You're hurt. Darling, sit down."

"I'm healing, it's just taking time."

"You don't look well. You're dripping obsidian on the carpet, love."

"I'll fix it."

"Let's fix you first. Sit." Hellin's shadow helped a mostly human-shaped shadow into an armchair. Jon stared, trying to guess at forms he could not make out.

"What happened?" Hellin asked. "You didn't send word."

"Because I didn't want to be overheard," the Doctor said. "It *is* an old enemy, but not Pratcherd, or Chauncellor, or Ash. It's older. Much, much older. Somehow it's *him*."

"You don't mean—"

"I don't know how it's possible, but I felt him out there in the darkness. I felt his mind, though I did not see his true shape. And he recognized me."

"But he can't even move, he's bound in Corestemar. Wouldn't we know if things had changed? The Seal would tell you."

"The Seal! I'll send word, see if he's well—" The Doctor's strange shadow shuddered.

"Wait. Healing first. You need to use your full mind for that, dear. Let's get you in one piece before making inquiries." Hellin's shadow reached for and grasped the shivering silhouette of a hand.

"Something with that creature's evil mind and presence was out there and it could see me. Too many people are suddenly able to see."

"Hush, love, focus on healing. That looks nasty. Can't I help?"

"I should have remembered to armor. I've been careless."

"I'm taking you to the infirmary tent. Can you walk?"

"Walk, yes, but I was lucky to find a horse to return here

on."

"Watch those near the lantern." Huge shadows like torn wings blocked out the light, and in a moment more there was nothing else to see, as Hellin took the lantern and led the Doctor outside.

Jon lay breathless on his cot, a million thoughts swirling through his head. *Doctor Blackfeather is not an archeologist. He isn't even human. What is he? A Guardian? Something else?* There were Shandorian legends of a time when creatures of an earlier world walked the land. The Ancients had built great cities, and Winged Ones had formed and leveled mountains with their power.

Jon fell asleep at last and had dreams of an Ancient warrior in liquid silver armor, who looked a little like Professor Sheridan, fighting a big monster with black wings in some golden limestone city very like the ruins they were excavating. The warrior lifted a hand with a silver object that Jon's sleeping mind told him was a pocket watch, and the monster made terrible hissing sounds. He woke up trying to sort memory from dream. Somewhere a tea kettle was whistling, and the reassuring smells of bacon and porridge told him he was awake and safe.

He told no one about what he had seen. He wondered briefly, seeing Doctor Blackfeather at breakfast, if he had dreamt everything. Doctor Blackfeather moved a little stiffly but looked altogether ordinary that morning, human and wingless. He explained that he'd been obliged to stay later with his inquiries than he'd meant to, and had just returned this morning. Only the Doctor's careful movements, and the way Hellin looked at him concernedly and touched his hand, told Jon that last night had not been all dream. Jon let the others tell about the adventure of the pickpocket.

"Well, you will have to content yourselves with causing your trouble in camp today," Hellin told them. "Corin and I have business in town."

"Again?" Djaren asked. "What about? Can we help?"

"You may help by staying here and deciphering those photographs," Doctor Blackfeather said gently. "If we cannot retrieve the stone, we will have no other clues to unlocking this place, or the Sharnish inscriptions. It will be all in your hands to save what has been lost."

Djaren beamed. "We won't let you down."

Hellin smiled. "That's settled then. I must gather a few things. I can trust you all to stay put here, can't I? I don't want you going wandering over the desert trying to track pickpockets. Not today, and I want a promise on that."

"We'll stick to the inscription today, I promise," Djaren said.

"We'll be right by the door all day," Anna agreed.

Jon nodded. "I'm very eager to interpret the Sharnish."

"And I'll guard them, don't you worry, Ma'am," Tam said.

"Thank you," Hellin said, picking up some things and packing them away in a bag. Jon noted some of the items as being rather suspect. When Djaren's attention was elsewhere, he saw Hellin slip a pistol case from the weapons collection into one large pocket, and into another she added a handful of what looked like copper bullets. She smiled at Jon warmly and touched his shoulder. "Don't worry about a thing, dear."

Jon blinked, and watched her and the Doctor carefully as they got ready to depart. When the Doctor passed the weapon rack, stopping for just a moment to rest leaning against it, the old black sword disappeared as he passed. The Doctor held only a cane, which Jon could not remember if he'd had earlier.

"Watch over them, Eabrey," Doctor Blackfeather told the Professor, quietly. "I leave them in your care."

The Professor looked worried. "Come back soon," he urged, "and safe."

"Don't you doubt it." Hellin patted her pocket.

They went off in the carriage, leaving the children waving after them.

"They aren't saying something. It's so thick you can nearly hear it," Ellea said, after they had gone.

"They'll be fine. Together they're invincible," Djaren told his sister. "No worrying."

Jon watched Djaren and Ellea. How much did they know about their remarkable father?

The other children went on ahead, down to the dig, but Jon lingered near the slower-moving Professor. All the questions in his head clamored for answers, even if they were awkward to ask.

"Sir? Where are they going? The Doctor and his wife, I mean." Jon asked.

"They are out looking for the stolen tablet. They will try to get it back."

"The way the Doctor got your satchel back?" Jon asked, watching the Professor's face for his reaction. The Professor looked at Jon, with an equally careful expression. "Rather like. Did you see something at the train station?"

Jon nodded. "I think I did. The thief took your bag, and then a man with wings flew down from the rafters after him. And they disappeared."

"Hmm," the Professor said noncommittally.

"I didn't say anything," Jon said. "I don't want people to think I'm crazy or tell stories."

"Is this the first time you've seen things that were, um, unexpected?"

"No, sir."

"Other things you've noticed, did they take place in Shandor?"

"Yes, sir." Jon was surprised to meet an adult who didn't give him a strange look about this. Jon had been keeping quiet about his observations and hunches as long as he could remember. The Professor just smiled a little, in an encouraging way, and Jon went on.

"I saw a carving move once. Tam didn't. And on a tour of the castle I saw a hallway Tam didn't, and later, a person no one else saw, who walked through a wall."

"I know the hallway," the Professor said. "What else?"

"I have hunches about things. Old things. Sometimes it's like they talk to me."

"And what sort of hunch do you have about Corin Blackfeather?"

Jon frowned. "Well he's not a thing, and he's not so old."

"You might be surprised at his age." The Professor smiled. "I mean what do your instincts and your gift say about him?"

"I want to like him, sir, but I keep seeing him as . . . odd."

The Professor sighed, and spoke softly. "I do not have the gift to see him when he shapes. I saw nothing at the train station, but I saw the token he left."

"The feather?"

"You saw that, too? Yes, the feather, and I guessed he would take care of things. Corin has taken care of me for a long time. His family took me in long ago, when I was in great need of help."

"There are more like him?"

"No," the Professor said. "Corin Blackfeather is the only one of his kind." He frowned, with some dark memory or pain. "The only good one. There were others, but not any longer. Not in our time."

Jon frowned, confused.

"It's not important," the Professor assured him. "What matters is that Corin Blackfeather can be trusted. He is as dear as a brother to me. I owe him my life. He knows, I believe, that you can see him, and it would seem he trusts you to keep his secret."

"I will, sir."

"Good." The Professor nodded.

"Do Djaren and Ellea know about him?"

"Much of it, yes," the Professor said.

"Sir?"

"Yes, Jon?"

"What is he a Doctor of? What is his degree in?"

The Professor grinned. "Being Corin Blackfeather. He never went to a university. His talents are a little too, ah, arcane, to merit a doctorate. But it sounds better on applications for dig site permits."

"But is he an archeologist?"

"Hellin is an archeologist. Corin—" The Professor paused. "Corin is a living piece of a more ancient world. He is not searching the past for pot shards. His specialization is in dealing with *other* things that have survived the centuries."

They had nearly caught up to the others now. Anna was pulling pictures carefully from her bag, and Djaren was trying to look at them all at once. Ellea stared at the door with her head tilted to one side, and Tam stood beside her in a similar posture. It looked funny. Jon smiled. The Professor looked, and smiled, too.

"Let's see about the photographs," the Professor suggested. "If you notice something, anything unusual, you can tell me. What you have is a gift, one I could wish I shared."

Together they set up a base in the corridor, under a sun shade. Anna pinned up all the pictures she had taken onto a large board. With the aid of a magnifying glass, a number of notebooks, and the Professor's expertise with languages, they were soon all hard at work trying to decipher the carvings.

First, Jon and Djaren set to work on translating the Alendi version of the text from the missing tablet. They worked at it, each taking a line at a time until they had a full translation written out in a notebook.

Djaren read it aloud. "Here lies the god-warrior, called stranger, called hero. Here with his armaments lies the one who slew the god Elush-bel-azzer. Sent from the heavens, from the far west, deliverer of Sharvor, came the god-warrior, servant of the One. Here he died, slayer of gods, slayer of terrors—"

"Rather long winded, weren't they?" Anna said.

"Shh," said Ellea.

Djaren continued. "—liberator of peace, he who felled the unworthy. Let none dare disturb his rest but his kin. Terrors await the unworthy. The abyss will swallow all his enemies. As the god-warrior slew Elush-bel-azzer so shall those who enter here be felled. A plague will fall upon them, and stones will crush their heads."

"Well, isn't that pleasant?" said Anna. "Makes you all excited to get in."

"Doesn't it?" said Djaren, missing her sarcasm.

The Professor looked equally starry-eyed. "We found the warrior's tomb. This is magnificent!"

"And think of all the words we now know of Sharnish, from the Alendi," Jon said.

"Plague and stones, yes. Very useful," Tam said.

Anna grinned at him. "Who's for something cool to drink?"

"I'll help you with the trays. I need to stretch my legs out," Tam said.

"Good luck with the languages. Don't translate anything exciting without us." Anna waved.

Several pitchers of water and plates of sandwiches had come and gone before any of the Sharnish had been translated. Djaren found another useful set of doubled lines around the newly cleared door frame that gave them three dozen new words. The sounds of workmen in other passages stopped, signaling the rest time, but the linguists kept working. Ellea played a little game with threads on her fingers, and Tam went to go look at the horses. Anna began another sketch of some interesting figures along the middle of the door. The workmen started up their hammering and digging again, and Tam joined them for a while, to have something useful to do.

"Do you know," Anna said after some time, setting down her sketch, "these figures might actually be words, too."

"They're a bit too detailed to be hieroglyphs," Djaren said, mopping his brow with an ink-stained handkerchief.

"I didn't say they were hieroglyphs, at least not an ordinary type. But see, all the little people are oriented toward the inset in the center. Two of them are pointing right at it, but there's nothing on it at all but a kind of star shape."

"I have something!" Jon exclaimed, standing up triumphantly with his notebook. "I've translated some Sharnish!"

"Let's see," the Professor said. Jon gave him the book, and the Professor read over it. "May the pilgrim/traveler of the west seek the sacred sign, and walk vigilant into the night. The moon's (horns?) will guide your way." He paused, and considered the door.

"There isn't any moon, not in the carvings," Ellea said.

The Professor looked at the door carefully. "That star, Anna, point it out to me."

Tam came back then, with another flask of water. "This lot is flavored with lime, Ma Darvin says. Anything new?"

"Yes," Jon said. "Shh."

"The star is right by your hand, see." Anna pointed.

The Professor dropped down to his knees and examined the spot closely.

"For such an ornate door, that bit looks a little empty," Ellea said, coming to stand nearer.

"It looks like a Shandorian Star to me," Tam said. "Four points, only this one is sideways, like an X."

"Professor," said Jon.

"Yes?"

"About the star. I have a hunch, sir."

"So do I." The Professor smiled. "Do you know, the Shandorian star is actually a symbol used often by the Ancients? It was sacred to them." The Professor put his hand out and touched the star with his fingers. Jon felt a shiver run down his spine. The star spun under the Professor's hand. The Professor stared, startled. The children jumped. The little figures along the middle of the door all changed. Where they had been was now an elegant flowing script in the language of the Ancients, interspersed with lovely, strange carvings.

The Professor read over them quickly, entranced, his lips moving. "This is amazing," he said at last, breathless. "They *were* here. This is their work. I believe the 'god-warrior' was in fact an Ancient, and died here, but others of his people helped to bury him." He looked up at Jon. "The original of that crudely wrought text above is right here. This is something. Something important."

Jon and the Professor exchanged glances. The Professor's eyes were shining. "This is an amazing find," he told them all. "I must send word to Corin and Hellin immediately. I will be right back. Stay here." He dashed off toward the camp, leaving the children staring at one another.

Tam pointed at the new carvings. "That's not normal, is it?"

"No," said Anna, looking perplexedly from her sketch to the new carvings.

"They say some of the carvings under the castle of Shandor move," Jon offered, a little uneasily.

"That's true," Djaren agreed.

"And some of them are invisible." Ellea nodded sagely.

"Right," said Tam.

"This *is* amazing," Djaren said, brushing the new lines with his fingers. "Jon, help me translate these. Ancient is harder than Kardu even. So many subtleties."

"I think this mark means 'Ascended'," Jon said.

"This one is 'Warrior'," Djaren added.

"And there," said Ellea, pointing to one new carving on the far left, "is the missing moon."

Chapter Eleven
Into the Tomb

Kara sat in the dirtiest, darkest tavern in the village of Alarna, surrounded by unhappy thieves.

"This is not good," Negal said, laying a nearly empty purse down on the table they shared. "These strangers are not good men."

"Good men do not hire people to do their thieving," old gap-toothed Himar said, pushing a cup of weak tea toward Kara. "Drink, little one. When you are bigger you can have something stronger." Himar was having something stronger.

"They took the stone, but what of us? They promised us payment, and we have received nothing." Negal slammed an empty cup on the table.

"You were promised," a terrible hissing voice said, from behind them, "a due reward when your work was done."

Kara tried to duck under the table, but a robed man's hand clamped down on her collar, hauling her up out of her chair. The dark-robed men stood at all the exits, keeping Negal's band of thieves trapped within. The tall rotting man advanced on Negal, part of his face visible in the dim light, partially desiccated, but oozing.

"Your work for me is not done," he said. "You have assembled the specialists I asked for, have you not? We will need them. I wish to open a door."

༄ ༄ ༄

"I think we can open this," Djaren said, looking at the door.

Jon examined the moon carving with great interest. It stood out from the door, and he could wrap his fingers around it. "I think this turns," he said.

"Maybe we should wait," Anna said. "The Professor will be back soon."

"He should have come back half an hour ago," Djaren frowned, looking at the fading light. "If we don't open this now, we won't have another chance until tomorrow." It was true. The workmen had stopped their digging and gone back to their tents for supper. The sun was low in the sky, and the Professor had not yet returned.

"I *do* want to see, even if it's just a peek," Jon agreed.

"We can close it again if it's boring," Ellea suggested.

"I can't believe that an Ancient's tomb could be boring," Djaren said. "Go on, Jon. Try turning it."

Jon glanced at Tam. Tam shrugged. Jon turned the moon. It gave easily under his hands, turning and locking into a new position. There was a visible crack now down one side of the door frame. Jon pulled. Nothing happened.

"Let me help," said Tam. Tam pulled. The door edged open a little more, with a loud scrape. Tam stood puffing.

"If we tied a rope about the moon, we could all pull together," said Djaren.

Anna fetched a rope and they fastened it around the horns of the moon. "If we break this, the Professor is going to be very upset," Anna warned them.

"We'll pull carefully," said Djaren, grinning, "and the Professor will be delighted to see that we found a way to open the door."

They all pulled together. After a long, difficult, sweaty time of heaving on the rope until their hands were raw, the door stood open a little over a foot. Anna had a lantern and matches ready, and the others all clustered around her as she lit the lantern and held it up.

They all peered into the narrow opening as footsteps crunched behind them.

"Professor, look, we've opened it," Djaren said, turning. He yelled suddenly, then, and the others turned too. The corridor was blocked by a group of men in dark robes, and some ragged villagers. One robed man had the pickpocket girl, thoroughly gagged, under one arm.

"You do not want to make so much noise," one of the men said, in a very odd voice. "If you make sounds, I will have to hurt one of your small friends." The speaker stepped closer, into the glow of Anna's lantern. His face, shadowed partially by his hood, was disgusting and rotten; teeth hung from a gray jaw dripping some kind of slime, and his nose was withered and sunken like a mummy's.

Anna dropped the lantern and clamped both hands over her mouth in order to stifle a scream.

"Good girl," the rotting man said. "Thank you all for opening the tomb. It was very clever of you. How would you like to see the inside?"

Robed figures pushed past the children, and hauled the door the rest of the way open. Jon grabbed Tam's hand, and Ellea and Anna grabbed Djaren's. Anna looked frightened. Ellea looked angry. Jon knew he must look petrified.

"I think it is time for my thieves to be useful," the rotting man said. "Two of you men, go first into the tomb."

One of the taller ragged villagers stood forward. "Apologies, lord, but first I would know what payment you propose to reward us for this work. You have made us many promises, but have yet to give us coins. We had a bargain."

"And I have a better one," the rotting man said, with a harsh, croaking laugh. He grabbed one of the villagers, a very old man with missing teeth and frightened eyes, and gripped him by the throat. Out from the flesh that the withered and rotting fingers gripped, blackness spread, with veins of sickly green. The old man's neck and face turned black, then his chest, and still the veins spread. He choked and his eyes rolled back. Red veins running across the whites turned to green and then to a slick and oily black. The pickpocket girl was kicking the man who held her, furiously. The rotting man dropped the old villager to the ground, where he fell without a sound, his head at an odd angle to his body, with some kind of dark slime oozing from beneath him. There was a terrible stench, from the fallen man and from the rotting one.

The other thieves all shrank away from the body.

"Do as I say, and I will not kill you," the rotting man said. "Two men. Go in."

"I don't know *what* you are," Djaren said, with uneven breath, "or who you are, but you *will* be stopped."

"How dramatic. So like your father." The rotting man gave him a horrible smile that showed his cracked lips, rotting teeth, and gray bloodied gums.

Anna closed her eyes.

Two of the thieves were pushed forward, and entered the tomb nervously. The others followed at a distance, with torches.

The tomb seemed to begin with a corridor of the same dimensions as the door. The thieves walked down it hesitantly into the shadows.

The robed figures followed the thieves, along with the

children, except for the six the rotting man directed to guard the door. Tam held onto Jon's hand so tight it almost hurt. Jon squeezed his hand back. He was glad to have Tam so near. He could see the pickpocket girl just ahead, slung over a robed man's shoulder. She looked angry, but scared too. She saw him watching her and scowled at best she could with a gag in her mouth.

There were cries up ahead and some of the thieves came running back. "The floor gave way around the corner! We have lost two men!"

"Then send on the next two," the rotting man barked. He turned a milky eye on the children and laughed. "Once we run out of thieves we will start sending you. The larger ones first. The small ones might not have weight enough to set off the traps."

"You are very bad," Ellea informed the rotting man. "I hope bad things happen to you."

The rotting man paused, considering the little girl carefully. "You have promise," he said. "Power, and promise. I wonder how you will grow up. If you grow up."

"Leave her alone," Jon said, surprising himself.

The rotting man fixed milky eyes on him next. "And you," he said, "are completely worthless. Too honest, too mortal, too innocent. Once I could have had a purpose for one such as you, but not now."

"Ignore him," Djaren hissed. "He's just a monster."

"My boy," the man said, "I am *the* monster. Didn't mummy and daddy tell you about me?"

Djaren glanced at the pickpocket girl, and then at the rotting man. "I guess they didn't think you were very important."

The man snorted. There were shrieks from up ahead, around another corner. Jon jumped.

"A blade came from nowhere," a man cried. "Both the men were felled."

"Has the blade stopped?" the rotting man asked.

"Yes, lord."

"Then move it, and send two more men on."

"Felled," Jon whispered, remembering something. "Terrors await the unworthy. The abyss will swallow all his enemies. As the god-warrior slew Elush-bel-azzer so shall those who enter here be felled."

Djaren drew in a breath. "Oh," he said.

"What are the next ones, again?" Tam whispered.

"Plague and stones," Jon whispered back.

"How does plague work?" Tam asked, puzzled.

"We don't want to know," Djaren said. "Ellea, Anna, close your eyes."

Something squished under Jon's foot. He did not look down. He closed his eyes. Tam held him hard. When there was yelling again Jon still did not open his eyes.

"That was unexpected," the horrible voice grated. "I thought the thieves would last longer. Untie the little one."

Jon's eyes opened. He looked for the pickpocket girl. She was being set down on the ground now. Her eyes were bright. It looked as though she might have been crying. "No," he said.

"Cowards!" Djaren yelled, starting forward. "You're going to send a little girl to go die? You're worse than a monster!"

Two of the robed men grabbed Djaren, stopping him from plunging toward the rotting man. It took three of them to restrain Tam. Jon lost his brother's hand, and clutched at the loose tail of his shirt instead. No one had grabbed him yet. Anna, along with Ellea, had two robed figures standing guard over her.

The rotting man looked at the children in some surprise. "My. You care about the life of a worthless child who robbed you. Do you think I care? Boy child, girl child, what are your kind to me, but ants upon the earth?"

The pickpocket spit out her gag, and snarled.

"Be careful!" Jon yelled to her. "Rocks will fall on your head!"

A robed man grabbed Jon now, too, and the pickpocket glared at him.

"The door said so," Jon added, desperately. The man who had a hard grip on both his shoulders was not rotting, but he didn't smell good either.

"Are you ready to surpass your ill-fated colleagues?" the rotting man asked the pickpocket girl.

She gave him a challenging glance, sharp chin high. "Try me."

Jon admired her bravery, but wanted to scream. He didn't want to see her die.

Djaren looked equally upset. Anna was crying. Ellea was frowning, and if looks could have killed, the rotting man would have fallen down dead a hundred times by now.

The pickpocket grabbed a torch from one of the robed figures, and stalked off down the hallway. She rounded a corner, and there was silence. The light from her torch had stopped moving. The men in robes waited. Nothing happened. There was still no sign.

ဢ ဢ ဢ

Kara crept along tight to one side of the passageway in the darkness, watching the ceiling closely. She left the torch immediately, and her eyes adjusted to the dark, as they always did. She noted a stone in the passage that stood out higher than the others, and the old and crumbling beams overhead that supported loose stones. *Not subtle,* she thought. She wondered if Negal's men had even seen the disasters coming. She shivered, and hugged the side of the passage.

Just let them follow me. I will make that walking corpse sorry.

She crept carefully to a point past the dangerous ceiling, and crouched waiting in the shadows. Robed men appeared at the end of the hall. They had found her torch. They advanced down the hallway. Kara saw the rotting man and the robed men with the children still hanging behind. The robed men moved closer. Kara held her breath. One of them stepped on the higher stone, and a large stretch of ceiling gave way. There were curses, screams and cries. Above it all, Kara heard the rotted man's laughter. "Well done, little thief. Was that your revenge? Shall I send in your playmates next?"

"Go ahead!" Kara barked back. "Let them try to find me."

Chapter Twelve
What was Found on the Warrior's Grave

Jon heard the pickpocket's voice echo down the passageway as dust settled around them. A rock had fallen and rolled not far from Tam's feet. Jon shivered and looked at the others.

"She's alive," Djaren said. "That's good."

Ellea was still frowning. The remaining robed men stood around them, looking with dismay at the fallen rubble and their comrades under it.

"Who shall I send after her?" The rotting man grinned at the children. One of his teeth was coming loose from his jaw, hanging by only a thread of flesh.

"Send me," Djaren said. He stood up straight, and faced the rotting monster, looking, to Jon's eyes, very brave indeed.

"No, no, young master *Blackfeather*." The surname was pronounced like a curse. "I have other plans for you." There was something dreadful in the way the rotting man said those words. Ellea gasped. She was staring at the rotting man with huge eyes, and a look of first horror, then hate. She whipped her head about to glare hard at the two men holding Djaren. First one and then the other took their hands off him, suddenly screaming. One ran back the way they had come, wailing, and the other fell to the floor, writhing and howling. Ellea and Anna's captors were next to begin acting strangely.

"No!" Djaren yelled, "Ellea, stop! No!"

Ellea, free now, glared across at the men holding Jon and Tam. One let go to begin striking at his own body, wildly. Another fell over in a faint.

"Run!" Tam yelled, pulling Jon along after him.

Djaren ran over to his sister and picked her up. "Never!" he told her, wrapping his arms around her, and running with her after Tam, Anna, and Jon down the rubble-strewn passage into darkness, away from the rotted man, and toward the pickpocket girl.

"Not for any reason. You know that," Jon heard Djaren's voice say, just ahead.

"You don't know. You don't know what he was *thinking*." Ellea sounded teary, and very frightened. "He is very bad. He is the worst thing ever. He wants bad things."

"We won't let him catch us, but you must never do that again. Father and Mother won't be happy."

"Stop!" The pickpocket's whisper halted them.

From the flickering torchlight behind them came the sound of the rotting man's rasping shouts.

"What is the next trap?" the pickpocket demanded.

"The door didn't say about any more traps," Jon said, breathlessly.

"Well, don't take another step forward. Your door is about to kill you," the pickpocket hissed.

Jon squinted in the dim light. "Step where?"

"We should light a candle. Does anyone have a candle?" Tam asked.

"I do, and matches," Anna said.

"Leave them in your skirts then," the pick pocket hissed. "We don't want to be a beacon to follow."

"But we can't see," Tam said.

"I can." The pickpocket sounded self-satisfied.

"And me," Djaren said. "We never got your name, miss, er . . ."

"I'm not a miss. It's Kara. Now if you can see, four eyes, make sure your little friends don't get us all killed. Step around that, and hug the wall. Show them, and follow me."

"Got it," Djaren said. He directed the others carefully around unseen dangers in the dark, and they pressed on after the girl, Kara.

Ellea and Anna held Djaren's hands, Tam held Anna's and Jon held Tam's as they traveled. Kara scouted ahead, telling them where to step, when to duck low under something, and where the turns were.

"We'll have to crawl, here," she hissed back. "Time to get your trousers dirty, presuming you haven't already."

"Very funny," Tam grumbled.

There was a tense spot a little later, where they each had to step in turn over some wire only Kara and perhaps Djaren were able to see. Ellea did it quickly and easily. Jon found the process nerve-wracking. Djaren and Kara walked him through it, then Anna. Tam's turn was last.

"Keep your head down, and step up, at the same time," Djaren said, sounding a little breathless. "Good. Now move your foot forward, straight, and keep your head ducked."

"Watch it!" Kara's tense voice ordered.

"I can't keep my balance like this," Tam said.

"I have your hand," Djaren said. Jon was disturbed by the note of panic in his voice.

"Careful," Kara whispered, also sounding scared.

"Foot forward," Djaren directed. "And down, now. Keep low. Second foot up. Keep it high! Now forward, and when I say, down. Good."

Kara let out her breath.

"That was good. Good job." Djaren sounded very relieved.

"Let's hope that runs the corpse out of minions," Kara growled. "Come on!"

They rounded another corner and abruptly stopped. Kara swore.

"It's a door," Djaren announced. "Our turn, Jon."

"Is it safe to risk a light now?" Anna asked.

"Fine," Kara said. "Just do this quickly. They're coming."

The flare of Anna's match illuminated all their dirty, frightened faces. She lit a long taper and held it up to a stone door, not entirely unlike the one that had led them here in the first place.

"Sharnish," Djaren said, "and Ancient. No easy languages, I'm afraid."

"I thought you were supposed to be clever," Kara said acidly.

"We can do it. It will just take time." Jon found his notebook in his pocket and squinted at the Sharnish words they knew.

There were shouts down the passage behind them.

"We don't *have* time," Anna said.

Djaren adjusted his spectacles, and frowned at the Sharnish letters. "Here falls, er, here *lies*, the god-warrior, stranger to the people."

Jon read the Ancients' script as well as he could. "Something, the humble, or is it small, servant of the One, fought and um, served well his job, er, mission."

"Get on with it," Anna urged, before Kara could interject first. Kara looked a little surprised.

"In rest forever, remembered as a hero, liberator of the age of peace," Djaren read. "I think. Slayer of Elush-bel-azzer."

"May he hold, or um, take a place among the, ah, ascendant, I think," Jon added, perusing the Ancient.

The sounds behind them were getting more disturbing, and ever closer.

"Hurryhurryhurry," Ellea whispered.

"Let none disturb the sleep of the god-slayer," Djaren said. "That's all. How can that be all?"

"The brother lies here with his weapons, er, arms. Let none disturb this sacred place." Jon looked up. "That's all."

They stared at each other is dismay.

A scream sounded quite close around the corner.

Kara threw herself at the door with an angry cry. The stone moved back an inch. They all looked at it.

"You just *push* it open?" Tam said. He set his hands against the stone and pushed. The door scraped open another inch. They all pushed together at the door then, as hard at they could. With their combined efforts, at last the door slid open wide enough for even Tam to squeeze through.

"Now shut the door again!" Djaren ordered, after just one glance about.

They all pushed as hard at they could from the other side and succeeded in settling the door back in its place. Tam slumped down to the floor to sit, breathing heavily. "That won't hold them," he said.

Anna lifted her candle, and the children looked around them. They were in a large room with no other exit. It appeared to be the tomb chamber of the ancient warrior.

"We need more light," Djaren said.

Anna dug in one large pocket and brought out a bundle of paint stained rags. "These are for my turpentine, they'll light fast."

Kara grabbed them from her and wound them around a stick of something she grabbed off the floor.

They had the makeshift torch blazing in moments, bright enough to light the whole room.

There was a large coffin in the center of the room, surrounded by the decaying rubble of a hero's burial. Bronze weapons were scattered on the floor, jeweled daggers and ornate spear heads. Flaking gold lumps marked ruined gilt chests and rotted wooden furniture. The air was old, and stale, but not as bad as Jon had read that the air in tombs could be.

"We shouldn't touch or tread on anything," Djaren said, eyes gleaming. "This is amazing. We have to document this."

Kara gave him a dirty look, and picked up a dagger. "We're being hunted by a living corpse with a fanatically loyal band of cultists. You want documentation. I want a weapon."

"Good point," Djaren admitted. "Right. Arm up."

Anna reached down and adjusted her skirts, pulling a very nice boot dagger from its sheath. "I turned thirteen last birthday, and got my knife," she explained, at Kara's surprised look. Tam found two sturdy old bronze swords. Ellea bent down to look at an enameled statue. Jon himself was drawn to the coffin. It was rectangular, and gray, all made of stone. It was covered in scripts and carvings. In the middle of the lid the Ancients' star was visible, encircled by the script of the Ancients.

"We have to block that door," Kara was saying.

"Hold this high, will you?" Djaren handed Jon the torch.

It was heavy, mostly something bronze. Jon held it as high as he could and stood beside the coffin, where he could light most of the room at one time. He peered at the writing, curious, while Djaren, Tam, Kara, and Anna shoved blades and spear heads into the cracks around the door, attempting to wedge it shut.

"He served the One with honor." Jon translated the words, and spoke them softly. "Let his brothers take up his memory, let his brothers take up his arms, and his shield. May his deeds be remembered and repeated in the war against the darkness. May those who come after be worthy."

Jon smiled. He had read the whole thing. He was getting better at this. He braced the end of the heavy torch on one knee in order to free a hand, and touched the star pattern. It unfolded under his palm. Something silvery and shining rose for a moment upon the stone, sending shivers through Jon's hand. He pulled away, startled, and the silver came away along with him. Jon turned his hand to look at what was sticking to it. There was a lacy silver emblem, about the size of a pocket watch, cupped in his palm. It wasn't a pocket watch though. Jon didn't know what it was, but thought he'd seen it before in a dream. While he watched, amazed, it melted into his skin. A light tracery of silver lines lay upon his hand as if someone had tattooed the emblem there. Jon stared.

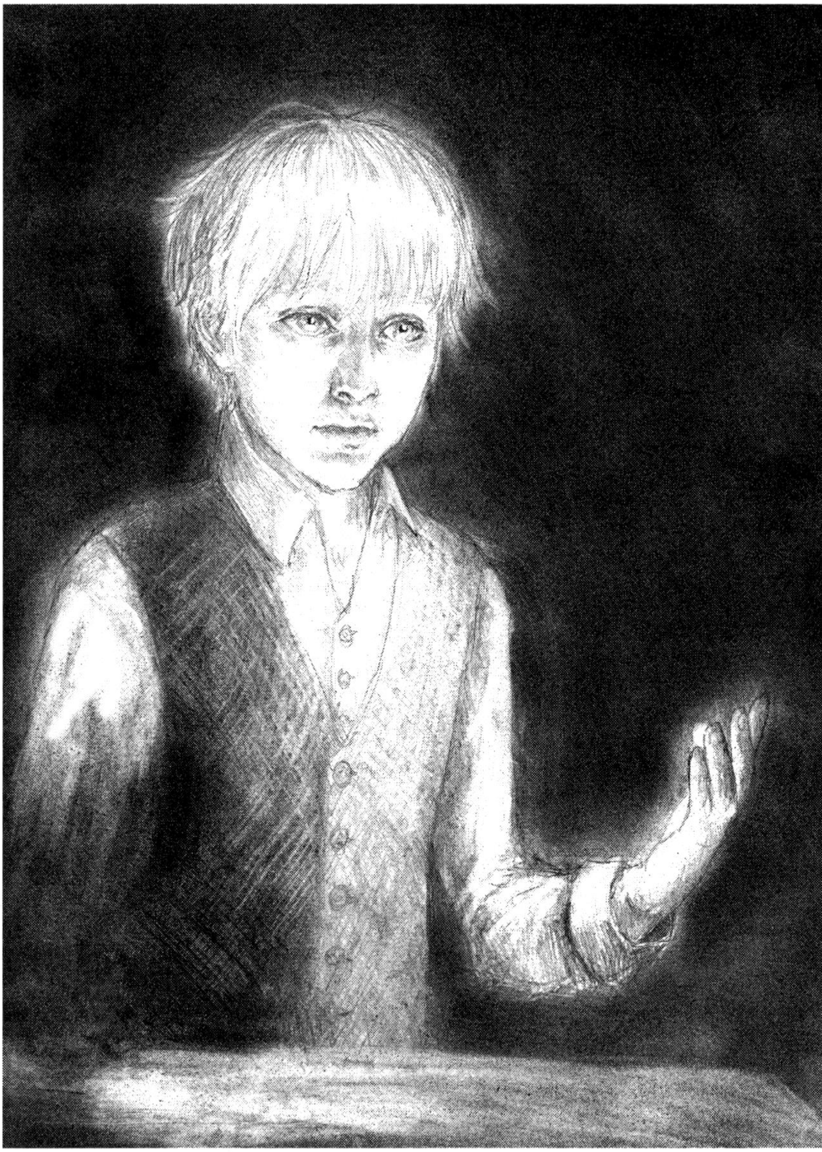

Chapter Thirteen
Against a Terrible Foe

"I said we need you to move, Jon," Tam was saying. Jon obeyed, still staring at the mark on his hand. Tam and Djaren pulled as hard as they could on the lid of the coffin. It slid slowly. Inside the coffin was a painted clay sarcophagus. Djaren and Tam hauled the stone lid across the floor, and with Kara and Anna's help began to wedge it against the door.

Jon flexed his hand. It felt normal, except for a slight tingle in his palm and in his fingertips. "Tam," he said uncertainly. "I touched something. I think I shouldn't have."

"Father will understand if we break some things," Djaren said, trying to lift the heavy slab to lean on the door.

"You just stay there safe," Tam added, helping with the other end of the slab.

A loud noise came from the opposite side of the door, and it shuddered and began slowly to scrape open. Anna shouted. The children tried to push the door back, to hold it motionless, but despite everything it scraped further and further open.

A robed arm reached through the widening crack. Kara stabbed it. There was a yell, but the men on the other side shoved the door open faster, making enough room for them to enter. Kara sprang to one side of the door and Tam, grabbing his swords, ran to the other. Tam hit the next man to come through square over the head, and he fell over.

Kara nodded at Tam with grudging respect and jabbed at the next man's foot.

The next thing to come through the door was a cloud of dust and debris, which took Kara and Tam by surprise. They stumbled back, coughing and rubbing their eyes, and before they had recovered, the rotting man had entered, with more of his men immediately behind. The rotting man took one look around the room, and his clouded, corpse-like eyes settled on the lid of the coffin. He looked from it to Jon, and his face twisted. Jon took a step back.

"You picked something up, didn't you?" the rotting man hissed. "Something not meant for children. Give it to me."

"I can't," Jon said, stepping back. He found himself with his back to the coffin.

"I will take it from you. Stand still and do not resist me," the rotting man said, reaching a withered hand toward Jon. The hand had only three fingernails on it, and they were yellow and cracked. One was falling off. Jon shrank away.

"No!" Ellea yelled, suddenly between them. She glared hard at the rotting man, and then looked surprised. She glared at him again, uncertain, and began to look scared.

"So very much promise. But you still have much to learn," the rotting man said, and stepped toward her.

Djaren leaped across the room and pushed Ellea out of the way. "Leave them all alone! I won't let you hurt them. You want me, fine, but you'll never hurt them. I'll stop you." He stood before the rotting man, bronze sword in hand.

The rotting man laughed, and reached out a decaying hand for Djaren's throat.

Kara stabbed the man then, from behind, with a wordless cry. He wheeled around and grabbed her with both hands before she could get away.

"No!" Djaren screamed, stabbing the man with his bronze sword. The rotting man ignored him. He did not even seem to notice. He lifted Kara by the throat, a gruesome smile on his cracked gray lips. Slick blackness oozed from his rotting fingertips onto Kara's skin. She struggled wildly. The rotting man's expression changed suddenly. The blackness was not spreading. There were no green veins, and Kara's skin did not change color under the rotting hands.

"You?" the man gasped. "Can it be? Are you the child?" His hood fell back, taking with it slimy clumps of dark hair, revealing a mottled scalp with peeling layers of skin and maybe even skull. "I have been searching for you, the one I lost." His voice had changed. It was still rasping, but the tones were soft and gentle, more disturbing that his shouts. "Beloved."

Kara's eyes were wide and horrified. Djaren's repeated stabs into the rotting man's back were having no effect.

With a strength Jon had never seen his brother wield, Tam brought the stone coffin lid down with a sickening crunch on the rotting man's head. He fell, dropping Kara, and lay buried under the slab. Green and black fluid oozed from under the stone.

The remaining men in robes stared down at the mess, turned their backs, and left without a word.

"Let's get out of here," Djaren said, grabbing Kara's hands and helping her to her feet. She was shaking.

The children followed the curving tunnels back out into the light, trying not to look too closely at the forms they passed. Kara had nothing sarcastic to say, and no one wanted to be the first to speak. Ellea held tight to Djaren's hand, and Jon stayed close to Tam. In an uncharacteristic display of concern, Kara helped Anna over the boulders in the section with the fallen ceiling.

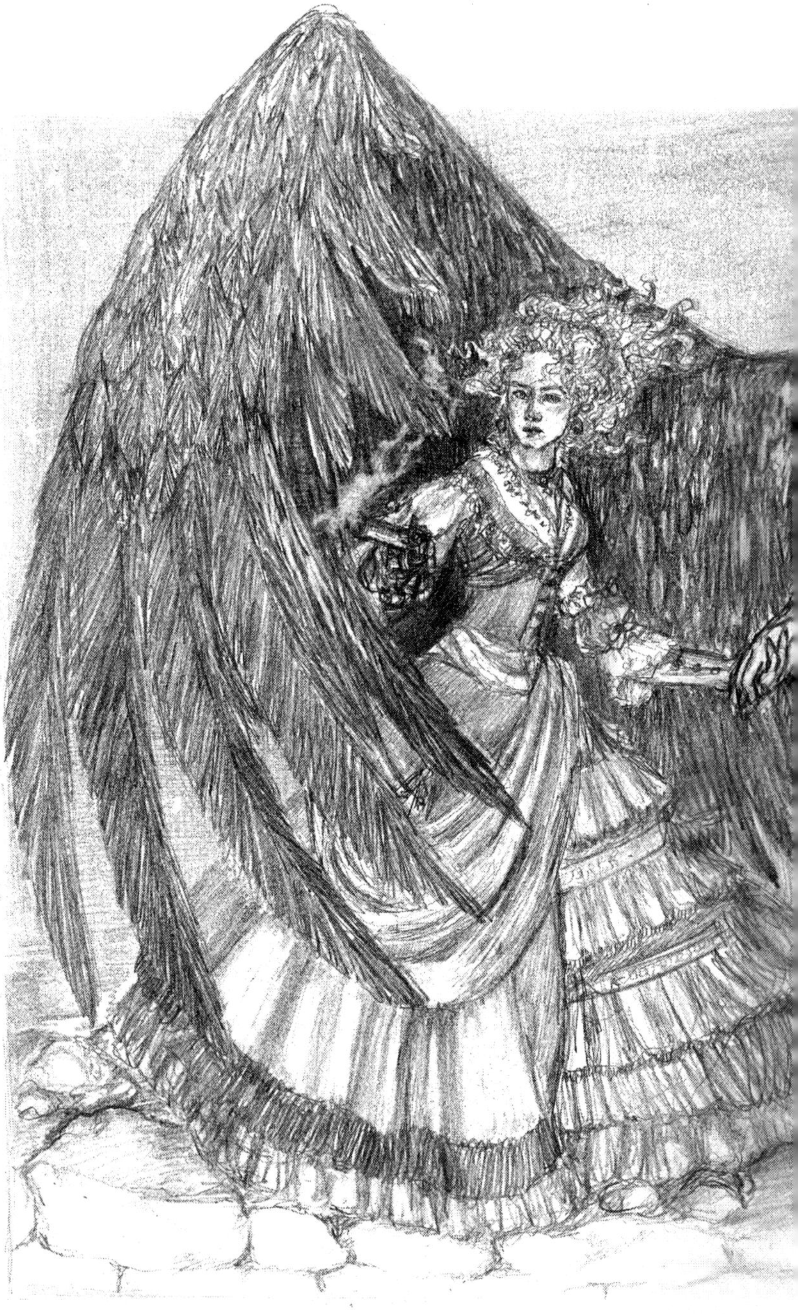

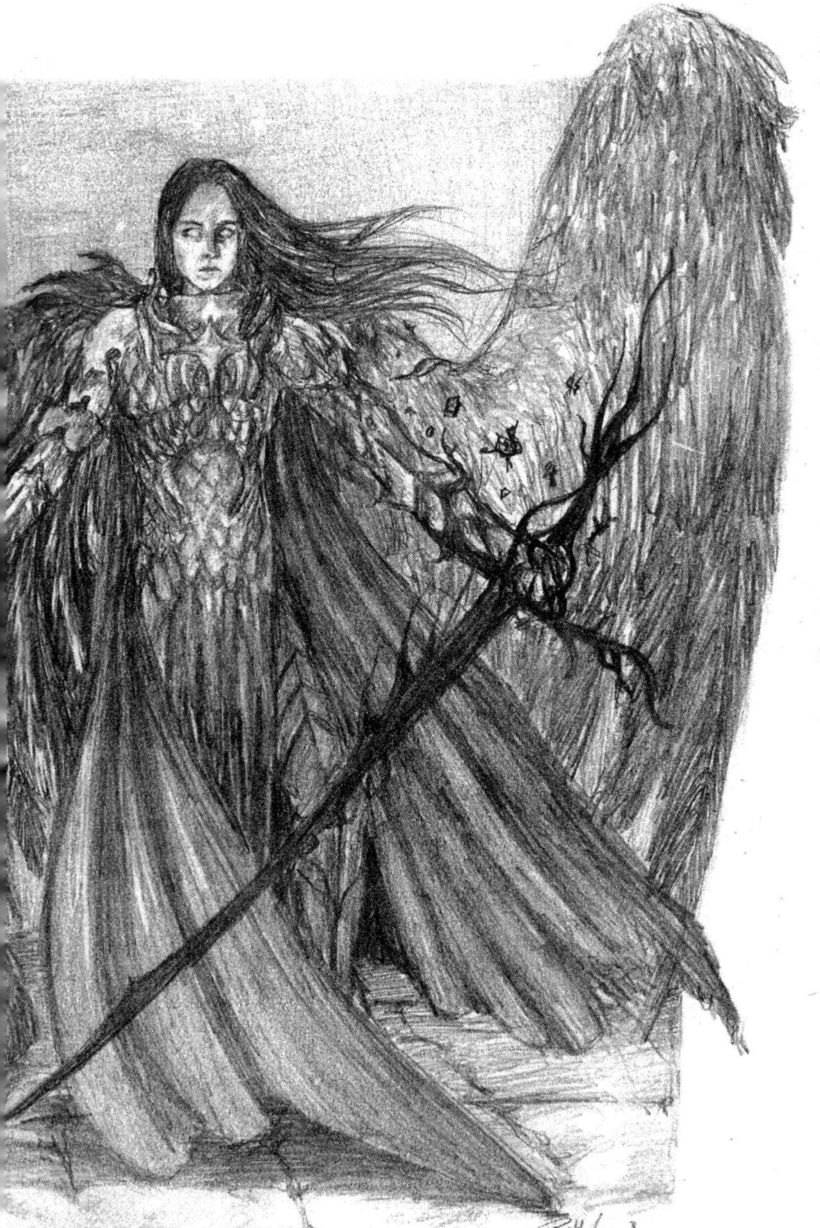

They emerged silent into the young night, to find themselves in the north corridor, beside the open door.

Stones rattled in the passageway ahead. Djaren made a sign, and the children stopped, listening.

"Professor?" Djaren asked.

"We have the man you call," an accented voice came from out of the shadows ahead. A robed man came around the corner. Four more men with torches followed him, holding the Professor, who was bound with ropes. His face was bruised, and blood trickled down from a shallow cut on his temple. He looked at them eagerly. "Thank the One, you're alive," he breathed. One of the robed men struck him. Djaren cried out in protest.

"We have orders," the foremost of the robed men said. "If the master rises, we follow his words. If the master does not rise, we slay this man, and take two of you to the holy temple. The rest we slay."

Kara reached into a pocket and pulled out the dagger she'd picked up in the tomb. "I can give orders too," she said. "I say we lay out a bunch of idiot cultists who lack the sense to think for themselves."

"Yes, Ma'am," Tam said grimly.

Djaren had kept his bronze sword with him, Jon noted. Tam pushed Jon behind him and Djaren did the same with a protesting Ellea. Anna stood beside Kara and gripped her belt knife.

There was a sound behind them. Jon and Ellea heard it first, then Djaren and Kara. They turned slowly to look back into the passage.

"That can't be right," Tam muttered, looking where the others were looking.

Lurching slowly into the torchlight came the rotting man. He was dragging one twisted arm behind him, and half his skull was shattered. His left leg bent oddly beneath him as he staggered forward, one unnatural step after another.

The children backed away, to find themselves surrounded again.

The Professor stared at the rotting man in surprise. "What is *that*?"

"We'd hoped you would know, sir," Djaren said, edging further away from it.

"I've never," the Professor began.

"Met me?" the corpse said. Its jaw didn't seem to be working properly, and its cracked skull was twisted sideways, but its speech was still understandable. "How soon children forget."

The Professor's brow creased. "No," he said softly.

There came a sharp, high, cracking sound and the corpse's "good" arm was blasted away.

All eyes went to the ledge overlooking the corridor. Hellin Blackfeather stood there, face lit in torchlight, form outlined by a sky full of bright desert stars, her copper hair flying loose about her and her pistol leveled now at the rotting man's head.

"Ma'am!" Tam cried. "Where's the Doctor?"

"Close," Hellin said. "Are you all well?"

Jon could see Doctor Blackfeather. He stood beside his wife, his huge black wings outstretched about her, forming even as Jon watched from the darkness of the spaces between stars, and the long shadows cast by torches. He wore armor of obsidian scales and held in one hand a strange sword of black nothingness that flickered and writhed like a flame.

Kara's open-mouthed stare informed Jon that she could see him, too.

"Yes, Lady Blackfeather," Jon answered. "We are now."

"Corin," the rotting man croaked. "Hellin, how nice to see you. I've so often wanted to visit. You do realize, Hellin, that your pistol is useless. This is not my real body."

"If it was, I'd say you were in a sorry state indeed. Who did you steal that from?" Hellin asked coldly. Her pistol hand did not change its aim.

"Does it matter?" the corpse cackled. "Do you remember, Corin lad, that it was nearly *you*, eighteen years ago? That would have been interesting." The rotting man looked right at the Doctor; he could see him too, though evidently the other robed men could not.

"And do you remember what we did to you, eighteen years ago?" Hellin asked.

"Every day," the rotting man said, spitting teeth. "Every hour. And I have come to exact my vengeance."

"And I thought you'd never get to the point." Hellin sighed.

"Always remember," the rotting man hissed, "it was you who stole something from me first." He turned and looked at the Professor, who was too stunned even to struggle against his captors. "You've eluded me for quite some time. He always found a way to hide you from me. You must remember me. It has been years, but years are the blink of an eye for your kind. Do you still have nightmares? Have you ever remembered your name? Or is that why you dig in graves, trying to find the people who forgot you, who abandoned you to me?"

The Professor was very pale. His scars stood out across his skin. "I have blocked you from my memories," he whispered. "I have forgotten you, and will forget you. You have no power over me."

"But we both know that's not true." The rotting man gave a hideous grin. "What is your name, Eabrey? What is your *real* name?"

One of the robed men pushed Eabrey away to join the children, and began to level a rifle at him. Hellin shot the man, with a crackling copper flash, but another man raised his rifle in turn and trained it on the Professor.

"Answer," the corpse man said.

The Professor swallowed. "I don't know."

The corpse grinned wider. "Because it is in *my* keeping. As are your children, Hellin," he said, looking up again at Hellin. He frowned, suddenly. Jon saw why. Doctor Blackfeather was no longer on the ledge. He was nowhere to be seen.

"Kill the scarred one now!" the corpse ordered. "At once!"

The Professor flinched. Jon grabbed his hand in both his own, wishing Doctor Blackfeather would act fast, wishing for a miracle. The tingle in his hand became a rush as something pulsed all through his arm, through his palm, and the Professor gripped his hand more tightly. Jon could not close his eyes, though he wanted to, as the robed figures all raised rifles to point at the Professor. Jon felt something odd, and saw a metallic gleam moving out of the corner of his eye. A sheet of liquid silver flowed up across the Professor's chest from their joined hands, as the first rifles barked.

Hellin was already firing her pistol at the rotting man. He fell to the ground but was still moving.

Something dark and shadowy flowed among the robed man, wielding a black flame like a weapon. Even as the rifles fired, they were sheared in the wake of the fury of Doctor Blackfeather. His eyes burned an unearthly glowing green, and his hair and robes billowed about him in an unseen, unfelt wind. Form after form was cast either into the walls, or up and out of the excavated trench altogether, thrown like straw dolls.

Bullets struck and bounced off the silver armor that covered the shocked-looking Professor. John found his own arm covered in the silver as well. It was cool, and molded to his shape.

The rotting man had taken cover behind the children, and Hellin was maneuvering for a clear shot at him. Kara dashed up to stab him, but before she could, his remaining broken limp arm twisted suddenly round and grabbed Djaren. Kara stopped, staring horrified first at Djaren's face, and then at the rotting man.

"Wait," the rotting man said to her, in what was almost a whisper. "I don't have much time left. Listen!"

Kara stood still, furious. Djaren met her eyes. His hand, still holding a bronze sword, moved a little. Kara saw. The rotting man didn't. He spoke quickly, impeded by his broken jaw. "I will find you. I will restore to you all that was stolen from you. I will give you back your destiny. You are meant to be so much more than this, Kara."

Kara threw her dagger at the same time as Djaren stabbed the man and Hellin got her shot at last. Bits of rotting man covered both Djaren and Kara. They stared at each other.

There were quite suddenly no enemies left to fight.

Jon, gripping the Professor's hand hard, looked up at him. The Professor was staring with wonder at his chest. A sheet of liquid silver armor covered the front of his body. Bullets were scattered at his feet. Jon began to release his hand, and the silver melted away. When Jon lifted his palm to examine it, the emblem there was very bright.

"What got the others?" Tam asked, looking up and down the corridor in confusion.

Doctor Blackfeather, wingless, unarmored, and almost ordinary, walked over the unconscious bodies. "The ones who did not flee, fell," he said. "It's over now."

Chapter Fourteen
Concerning Gifts and Legacies

"I'm confused," Tam said. Jon gripped his brother's hand in his unmarked one and stared at the mess around them.

Hellin leapt down into the corridor, where Doctor Blackfeather caught her with practiced ease and set her down. She left his arms to gather Ellea and Djaren close to her in a hug. Jon was caught up next, along with Tam, and then the still shaky Professor. "I'm sorry, dears, he was never meant to come here," Hellin said, breathless. "He won't bother us again."

"I'll make sure of it," Doctor Blackfeather said gravely. He set down a large black antique sword—not a tool of flame and void—against the corridor wall and grasped both the Professor's hands in his own. He looked the Professor over, worriedly. "How are you unharmed? I didn't make it to you in time." Doctor Blackfeather looked even paler than usual. He grabbed the Professor in a hug, while Hellin caught up Djaren and Ellea a second time. "I am sorry, little brother. I never thought he could find us, find you. I'm sorry, so sorry, Eabrey."

"I've got you," Hellin told her children. "He's gone. He's gone now."

Ellea buried her face in her mother's hair. Djaren submitted to the second hug for a moment, but then pulled away, to stand beside his father.

Jon accepted his second round of hugs without complaint, feeling shakier now that he was safe than he had when everything was terrible. He didn't want to cry in front of people.

"That was not a rival archeologist." Tam stated, looking at

the mess on the ground.

"No," the Professor agreed, his voice still shaky. He stared at the pieces of the rotting man.

"I have enemies," Doctor Blackfeather said. He sounded weary. Djaren looked up at him, and father and son locked eyes.

"Enemies with severe leprosy?" Tam looked skeptical.

"Something like that."

Hellin was not content until she had examined the Professor for bullet holes. The silver armor was entirely gone, leaving no trace of its existence but the ruined bullets on the ground.

"I'm fine," the Professor assured Hellin. "It was quite a remarkable experience. I think I owe Jon here my life. And he may owe us some valuable information. Whatever did you find in that tomb?"

Jon shrugged, suddenly nervous under so many eyes. He lifted his hand, and the silver lines on his palm lit and gleamed in the torchlight.

Doctor Blackfeather frowned at it. "We'll look at this later, indoors, and in the light."

Tam took Jon's hand and lifted it to have a look. "Does it hurt?" he asked, making a face. "Can you peel it off? We could try soap."

"It tingles sometimes," Jon said. "It was on the tomb lid, with an inscription. The writing is still there. I don't know how to take it off. Will Ma be mad, do you think? I didn't mean to pick it up. I'm sorry. Are you very angry, sir?" He looked up at the Professor.

The Professor met Jon's eyes and shook his head. "It chose you. These things don't happen by accident. And with it, you saved me. I am not angry."

Doctor Blackfeather frowned and looked over the emblem. "Well, *sometimes* by accident." He smiled a little ruefully. "But there always seems to be a greater reason beyond. Regardless, Jon, you saved my brother, and for that, I and my family are grateful to you."

"Accidents? Oh, the Seal," Hellin murmured. "We should certainly make sure that he's safe, too."

"He would know about things like this." Doctor Blackfeather indicated Jon's palm. "And I need to talk to him about how *that* got into a body, and found us here." Doctor Blackfeather looked at the ground with distaste.

"Sir," Jon said. "Bad things happened to people in there," he gestured toward the door. "I don't know if anyone's . . ." He trailed off.

Doctor Blackfeather met his eyes and nodded. "I will see if there is anything that can be done. Anyone in need of aid will have it, do not fear."

Hellin glanced at the Doctor. He nodded at her, and then disappeared down the dark passageway.

"Let's go inside, and away from this," Hellin said, guiding Jon and Ellea before her, back toward the tents. "We'll discuss this and Jon's discovery over tea."

Ellea glanced at Jon. "I think your new thing is very pretty."

Jon blinked at her. She slipped her small hand into his, and together they processed back to the tents, and tea.

ဢ ဢ ဢ

Kara lagged behind, unsure, still looking at the scattered remains of the rotted man. Djaren stayed, too, until the others were a little further on.

"Why didn't he kill me?" Djaren asked her, softly. "He could have. He just talked to you."

"How should I know?" Kara said. "Whatever he thinks, um, *thought*, I don't know him. I'd remember."

"What do you think he meant, he'd find you?"

Kara shivered. "He was a crazy dead man. What do you think he meant about plans for *you*?"

Djaren frowned, and suppressed a shiver himself. "He was probably just crazy. And um, sick. Father, who was he?"

Kara glanced up, alarmed, to see that the burning-eyed beautiful dark angel-turned-nobleman was standing near, a little too tall and too pale for a human, even in his current form.

Doctor Blackfeather laid a hand on his son's shoulder. Kara kept her distance from the Doctor, circling him slowly, looking for where he kept his wings. He might be pretty, but he wasn't *right*.

"That is some unfortunate man who surrendered his will to an evil," Doctor Blackfeather said. "What spoke to you was something else."

"But who was *he*?"

Doctor Blackfeather frowned. "An old evil that should no longer be in this world. I had hoped he could never bother us. He has learned some new tricks."

"Will he come back?" Djaren asked.

"Not if I have anything to do with it," the Doctor said. His face was grim. Kara caught the glint of unearthly green fire in his eyes.

"And what are *you*?" she asked him.

He paused, and considered her carefully. "What we all are; whatever we make of ourselves."

"That's not a full answer."

"It's the answer I am giving you."

"Back there, there wasn't anyone to save, was there?"

He shook his head sadly. "The healers have arrived, but I do not think their skills are equal to the task they have. They will try."

"To help tomb thieves," Kara was skeptical.

"To help the people whose past we have been allowed to uncover. We are here by permission of the people. Without the people's good will, we lose all we have done here. I do not want the ill will of the village. Tonight's tragedy serves no one."

Kara frowned at the ground. "You're not supposed to care," she muttered.

"Because if we care, you might need to?" Djaren guessed.

"Shut up," Kara told him.

Ahead, the others had paused. "Come along," Hellin called, "Let's get everyone inside and cleaned up."

"Look," Kara said. "It was strange and everything, but I'm leaving you freaks and your enemies."

"Not until after you've had some tea," Hellin called back. "Corin, do enforce that, will you?"

Kara looked up at the pale avenger dubiously. She couldn't outrun something otherworldly with wings. She hesitated, looking from adult to adult with distrust.

"You saved all our lives," Djaren said quickly.

"You did," Anna added, coming back to smile at Kara, "and we'd never have made it through that passage without you."

"Then we owe you a reward," Doctor Blackfeather told Kara.

"What kind?" Kara looked at him with suspicion.

"Let's start with tea, and talk about it from there."

"Don't you have anything stronger?" Kara asked, falling into step beside him.

"We made rather a mess of the tomb, Father. I'm sorry," Djaren said.

"Oh dear," the Professor said, overhearing, as they caught up to the waiting group.

"I would rather have you in one piece than all the treasures of the Ancients," Doctor Blackfeather said.

༄ ༄ ༄

The camp was stirring as they returned. Harl and Ma Darvin met them anxiously, and pulled Anna immediately into a mix of hugs and scoldings for not coming home for dinner. Brief explanations were given, and a late tea was assembled in the sitting room. Jon thought of the rotting man and was unsure he would ever have an appetite again.

Doctor Blackfeather placed the battered black sword back in the weapons case and took a seat across from Jon. "Let me see your new 'shield' closer in the light."

Jon extended his hand, palm up. "I don't know how to put it down, sir. I keep trying."

The Professor sat nearby and leaned over Jon's hand again, fascinated. "This is the craftsmanship of the Ancients, certainly, and in perfect working order. It is unlike anything we've found, though."

"It seems to have fused with you," Doctor Blackfeather said. "Try willing it out."

Jon tried, uneasily. Nothing happened. "I don't know how to work it."

"It may only work when you really need it. With practice,

you may learn to guide it with your thoughts," Doctor Blackfeather said.

"But I can't keep it!" Jon said. "Not in my hand. This is a priceless artifact, isn't it? You just said it was work of the Ancients."

The Professor looked thoughtful. "I can't think of a worthier bearer for it. If it chose you, then I cannot argue with its choice."

Doctor Blackfeather met Jon's eyes. "You will have to keep it a secret. And it may attract unwanted attention. This will be both a gift and a responsibility for you to bear."

"The rotting man knew I had it," Jon said, worried.

"Then we will protect you," Doctor Blackfeather said gravely. "Regardless, you will be safe from that *particular* danger in Shandor. There are borders that it can't cross."

"But sir, I want to be an archeologist. I want to see places, and find things."

"I think you have a gift for that," Doctor Blackfeather said. "If you do not object, I would be honored to have you and your brother stay under my care and protection next summer. You have a gift for languages, for mysteries, for seeing, that would be a great asset to us, here and wherever we dig next."

"Do you mean it, sir?" Jon could feel a wide smile on his face.

"He's willing to face ancient evils, endure heat and dust and tomb thieves for a chance to dig up pot shards and old letters." Hellin smiled. "He must be one of us."

Tam sighed. "Well, you know I can't let you do all that without me looking after you. I promised Ma I would. Though how I'm going to explain about the thing you got stuck in your hand, I don't know. I've been scared half to death all night. Is this really what you want, Jon?"

Jon nodded, looking from his brother to Djaren and Ellea. "I like it here. With you."

Kara, caught trying to pocket a crystal brandy decanter, snorted. "Weird happy family. Good for you. I'm leaving."

Hellin took the decanter from her, patiently. "I don't like thinking of you out there with no one to look after you."

"You're the people the walking dead are after," Kara said. "I'm safer by myself, thank you."

"But what he *said*—" Djaren objected.

Kara shot him a warning look. "I don't need your band of freaks to call attention to me. I have a life."

Doctor Blackfeather looked at Kara. She looked back suspiciously.

"I would like to buy a watch from you," he said.

Kara frowned.

Hellin reached into a vase near her elbow and drew out a bag of coins. "And the statuette in your sleeve please. I'm rather fond of that one, and you'd never get a fair price for it in town."

Kara glanced from one of the Blackfeathers to the other, and emptied her pockets, grumbling. The contents were rather amazing, and included the Professor's pocket watch, Tam's bag of coins, a silver-edged bookmark of Jon's, a comb of Anna's, and a bracelet Jon had seen a while ago on Ellea.

"Keep the bracelet," Ellea said. "I dropped it for you, because you'd lost yours."

"Did not," Kara grumbled, pocketing the bracelet again.

Hellin handed Kara the bag of coins, and Kara glanced into it, surprised. "What kind of trick is this?"

"My bad habit of mothering," Hellin said, handing Kara a clean handkerchief and a hairbrush from a nearby table. "Do stay for dinner."

Kara gave Hellin a dubious look. Djaren grinned, trying not to laugh.

"Shut up," Kara told him.

"You may keep the dagger too," Doctor Blackfeather told her softly, on the way to dinner. "You choose a dangerous path. If you need help, my family owes you a debt."

Jon grabbed Kara's hand and squeezed it. "Thank you for helping us."

Kara shook him off. "Don't get that thing on me." Her look said something nicer than her words, and Jon smiled, answering that.

Chapter Fifteen
A Few Words in Parting

Kara stayed for dinner and resisted the temptation to pocket any more of the interesting trinkets that passed before her. She refrained from commenting that the food was too bland, and she didn't stare at the scar-faced man's scars or at the winged freak's lack of wings. She even remembered to use the wooden tableware instead of her fingers. Being polite was much more difficult than she'd anticipated.

After dinner it was quite late, and Kara was determined not to lose any more time, in case the lady realized just how much silver was in the bag of coins she'd handed over.

She crept to the door unnoticed, and was about to slip out, when Jon saw her and dashed after her. "Are you going?" he asked. She considered pointing out to him what a stupid question that was, but he stood blinking up at her with his huge blue eyes as if she were someone he respected to a painful degree. The scar-faced Professor had followed him and was looking at her, too.

"Take care of yourself, half-size," she told Jon. "Hey, um, you with the scars. What does your watch say?"

The Professor blinked at her, surprised. "Oh. Um, it's an inscription, from an old friend." He opened the recovered watch and held it out.

Jon read it aloud for Kara. "Mortal or immortal, always treasure time. Herringbroke."

"What's that supposed to mean?" Kara asked.

"Just what it says," the Professor said, softly.

"Which are you, then, mortal or immortal?" Kara said

mockingly.

The Professor said nothing, just brushed his hair behind one of his odd ears self-consciously, with a glance at the floor. "I don't know."

Kara was suddenly sorry she'd asked. "Well, you're all freaks together. Good for you. I'm leaving."

"Take care," Jon said. "We'll miss you."

"And you're the strangest of them." Kara said, mussing his hair. "Don't ever cross my path again."

She left without looking back. She walked through the dark, swearing when the moon disappeared behind cloud, but able to see, regardless. As it got chillier she pulled her coat closer about her. She had only trudged a few miles toward town when the sound of a carriage caught up with her.

"Momma thinks we're asleep," came Ellea's whisper. "So hurry and get in, and don't argue."

Kara considered arguing anyway, but was too tired to think of anything particularly stinging, and so with a single curse she pulled herself up onto the carriage.

She climbed to the top to find Djaren in the driver's place and Ellea making room for her beside them.

"We couldn't let you go without saying goodbye," Djaren said. "And we do need to talk."

"What about?" Kara frowned.

"You're unkillable by whatever that thing was, you can see in the dark as well as Ellea and I, and can break locks by kicking them," Djaren said.

"How do you know—?"

"And you see Poppa," Ellea added. "And I can hear you clear as talking when you think too loud."

"And a monster who is after us is also after you," Djaren said, before Kara could interrupt. "You're a freak just like us. I won't ask any questions, but I say we make an alliance. We're going to be in Germhacht next May, to go ask the consul for permission to dig in Narmos."

"There's supposed to be a temple there that's over three millennia old," Ellea said.

"It will be great fun. You should come."

"Will there be another attack by supernatural horrors?" Kara asked sarcastically.

"Only if we're lucky," Djaren grinned at her. "Promise you'll come."

"I don't make friends."

"Then be our arch-enemy. Just come."

"You are an insane boy, and I should have broken your face and spectacles long ago now."

"So you *will* come."

"Good-bye." Kara hopped off the carriage as it passed the first of the farms outside the village, and took to her heels, with Djaren's silver spectacle case tucked carefully in her breast pocket. It had a star on it.

ஐ ஐ ஐ

Jon found the rest of the summer to be glorious if uneventful. Professor Sheridan had been nauseated, Hellin told them, seeing the mess in the passage, and even sicker at the sight of all the smashed artifacts in the burial chamber. Once he settled down to cataloguing and documenting, however, he was much happier. Djaren and Jon helped with translations and Anna with sketches and photographs, and work progressed quickly at the site. One day, not long before the end of Tam and

Jon's time in Alarna, it came time to open the clay sarcophagus and see how the Ancients and the Sharnish peoples had buried the warrior. They stood gathered about the sarcophagus in hushed silence, as Harl and Doctor Blackfeather carefully lifted the lid. Anna held up a lantern to reveal the inside. Funeral wrappings lay bundled in an otherwise empty case. There was no sign at all of the warrior.

"I thought not," Doctor Blackfeather said softly. "He joined the Ascendant."

The Professor spoke a blessing and touched the grave clothes. They crumbled under his light touch.

"They haven't been here for well over two thousand years, Eabrey," Doctor Blackfeather said, going to his side.

The Professor looked pained. "I know," he whispered. "I just hoped that perhaps they had left a sign. Something."

"They did," Jon said, lifting his hand. The Professor took the offered hand and stood, looking again at the silvery emblem.

"And they passed it to you," the Professor said, with a sad smile.

"What kind of sign are you looking for?" Jon asked, watching the Professor's blue eyes intently.

"One of life," he said, wistfully. "Come along. We have work to do."

ಸಿ ಸಿ ಸಿ

The *Times* came the next day, as they sat waiting for the train that would take the Gardner brothers home. The children sat gathered round Anna as she finished the serialized story aloud.

Djaren held out his hand and Tam grudgingly set a coin in it. "Three more faints. I was right." Djaren grinned. "And she didn't die, Ellea."

Anna made a face at them. "She accepted Lord Ellerton's proposal of marriage, and fell into his arms. They're going to live happily ever after."

"Until she dies in three months," Ellea said.

"Maybe she doesn't. Maybe now she's done falling in and out of love with people and caring for her mad aunt and ailing father, she'll steady out a bit and not feel the need to pitch over so often," Tam said soothingly.

Ellea shrugged. "Less interesting."

"There'll be a new story next month," Djaren said. "And a new dig next spring."

"I can't wait," Jon smiled. "I have a lot of reading to do about Narmos."

"Hmm," Hellin said. "Narmos isn't somewhere either I or your mother want you reading too much about. Corin and Eabrey will be overseeing most of the digging, and we'll be camped a bit further off."

"Are you saying Narmos isn't safe?" Djaren asked, looking excited.

"History is never entirely safe, love. You're old enough to know that. In history we find ourselves, the demons we have overcome, and the things that make us as we are."

"I thought history was mostly meant to be boring," Tam said.

"That's the common misconception," Hellin said. "Here's your train coming."

"Where's Doctor Blackfeather?" Tam asked, looking around. "I thought he said he might be traveling with us."

Jon watched with a breathless smile as a winged form

alighted on the top of the moving train, cloak and wings billowing in the hot wind. "He will be."

Hellin put a hamper of sandwiches into Jon's hands and smiled at him. "You'll be safe all the way back home."

"I'll be going along as well," the Professor said. "I've got a book or two waiting for me at Merigvon."

"And next summer, we'll be camped near the city of the Invincible Kings, whose power allegedly came to them from the elder gods of Narmos. They were said to smite down their enemies with lightning and plagues, until the entire civilization was destroyed by natural disasters. Only a few escaped its ruin and fled clear across the world, bringing their story with them."

"And you will not be digging at Narmos," Hellin said. "Your father will."

Djaren grinned at Jon and Tam. "We're going to have an exciting time. We'll see you next spring."

"This might come in handy," Ellea said, taking Jon's hand in her own, and lifting it to see the sparkle of silver again.

"It won't have to," Hellin said again. "So don't you worry, dear. Here's your passenger car now."

The Professor guided them up the steps and Tam carried the luggage. Jon paused to look back at Anna and the waving Blackfeathers and grinned. "Thank you. For everything."

"Aye, it's lovely you have a treasure of the Ancients," Tam grumbled, pulling the cases up the steps, "But what's Mum going to say?"

Writer and illustrator **Ruth Lampi** lives in Philadelphia with her best friend and editor, Jessica. They share several literary worlds, three cats, and all their adventures. Ruth and Jessica have been writing about Shandor and its denizens since they were teenagers growing up in Wisconsin.

Look for the continuing story of the Blackfeather family and their friends at www.worldofshandor.com.